W9-CYW-095

Bridge to
Paradise

ALSO BY FAITH SHANNON . . .
The High Road

Bridge to Paradise

by Faith Shannon

ZONDERVAN PUBLISHING HOUSE
GRAND RAPIDS, MICHIGAN

To my son, Philip Shannon,
and friends Elsie Young and Mr. Al Bryant,
without whose counsel this would not have
been completed.

Bridge to Paradise

1

SHE WAS ALONE in the rear of the old mansion. Thick carpeting carried her soundlessly upstairs. Lynn ran down a hall, muffled sounds from below adding to her fear. She must hide! They were following her!

She stopped by a door, quietly turned the knob, and stepped through, closing the door behind her. She edged along the wall to a heavily curtained doorway and parted the curtain at eye level.

Through dusky vapor, a girl walked past. She seemed in a stupor, eyes closed, hands outstretched, as though groping for something in a dark world of fantasy. A boy, lying on the floor with hands over his eyes, laughed — a high, uncanny laugh that shot needles through her veins.

Footsteps again in the hall! Lynn's heart raced wildly as the latch clicked. As the hall door opened, she slipped around the curtain and flattened herself against the wall, watching the shadowy figures in horror. The flowered curtain moved and a tall man glanced around. Lynn sank to her knees by a large hassock and tried to blend into the scene; she didn't breathe again until he had disappeared.

A strange fragrance floated in the vapor; there was the same group sitting in a circle on the bare floor staring at burning candles. The air was layered with heavy incense. Was she still in the house where they had first taken her? Was this scene real — or was she dreaming?

Lynn tried to hold her eyes open, but she was so tired; it was hard to keep alert. She let her head drop to one side and leaned her face against the hassock; the velvet was soft. It became a grassy slope in Fairmount Park, the incense coming from flowering shrubs along the parkway. Joel was stretched full-length on the ground, his black, wavy hair floating across his books. Strange that it was dusk; they usually came here after school in bright sunlight.

Strange — how the exact sensation of those wonderful moments with Joel returned.

He took her hand in both of his and his brown eyes held hers with a look she had never seen before. His voice drifted slowly: "Lynn, I can't keep from saying this any longer. I love you. I've loved you since we first met two years ago. Remember the first time you came to our youth group? You must have been homesick for Virginia. You looked so alone; I wanted to stay close beside you always — and — well, I never felt like that about any girl. Darling, do you care — do you think of me in the same way?"

Lynn's answer leaped from her eyes. She whispered, "Oh, yes, Joel, I do," her throat aching with emotion. In the background Bernice was yelling, "Lynn, Lynn! Where *are* you?"

She jerked and threw herself down in the grass. It wasn't a park! It was a room swaying in layers of color. Why was she here? How did it happen? *Joel, my darling, I'm lost! Lost Lost!* The words echoed in the dim recesses of her brain.

Far away a voice sounded, ringing louder and louder in her ears. "Paging Miss Hale. Paging Miss Hale . . . ."

She was lost! The crowded station engulfed her. Thousands of strange faces. She felt like crying but couldn't because she had to keep thinking fast. Bernice's letter told her to stand by the Information Center. It seemed she stood there for hours; the lostness was terrifying. She hated the city.

The voice rang louder: "Paging Miss Hale, Miss Lynn Hale. Paging Miss . . . ." Slowly she turned to answer the call.

She stood on shaky legs in a phone booth. Bernice didn't sound as gay as she had in Virginia. She clipped out a curt message, "Catch the subway downtown. There's nothing to it. All you have to do is . . . ."

But I've never been to Philadelphia before! Nausea threatened.

She asked first one, then another, and finally made her

8

way to the right street corner. The milling crowd swept her down a stairway and through a turnstile.

Lynn gasped, "How much?" reaching for her purse, and a woman in the booth snapped, "Twenty-five cents!" A girl shoving from behind sneered, "Stupid. Can't you read signs?"

She staggered through the train doors. No seat. The car lurched; the grinding screech of the wheels pierced her ears. The crowd shifted, pressing them all like leaves in a giant press. They flew through space, swaying back and forth until lights showed a station. The train ground to a swift stop; people rushed in and out. Shrieking on through the black tunnel, car lights blinked on and off, on and off. Black and white tiles rushed past at each station, each sign splashing a name too fast for her to read.

What was the next stop? Someone said *Ogontz*. That sounded like the one.

Bernice was there to meet her. She wasn't smiling, but came up, kissed her lightly on the cheek, and remarked, "Well, you made it. Where's your luggage? Did you check it to the downtown station?"

And her own answer sounded hollow and far away. "I asked them about it, but they couldn't locate mine. One man said it might take another day."

"That's nice, I must say!" Bernice became irritable. "If you had checked at Baltimore, this wouldn't have happened."

2

"WOULDN'T HAVE HAPPENED — wouldn't have happened."

The words ricocheted, and Lynn stirred uneasily. She awoke, startled by a clap of thunder. Lightning seared the room, turning the group to weird silhouettes around the amber candles.

Lynn's head rested on the hassock, but she kept her eyes

9

open. *These are real people — not spirits melting into air. This is something I am living through now! How did I get here?*

She tried to organize her thoughts; they evaded her. With great effort, she concentrated on those last words.

Wouldn't have happened. Oh, yes. That was when Bernice met her at the subway station in Ogontz. Lynn would never forget. The memory of that first day in the city was branded on her heart for a lifetime.

They were not glad to see her. Her father did not greet her with his usual bear hug. His hollow words, "What are the tears for, Lynnie? You're here now; this is your new home," crushed her sudden joy at their reunion.

That house at 36007 was not her *home.* Home was back in Virginia in the Blue Ridge. But the house on Magnolia Hill had been empty since Mother died. Her father had left Aunt May in charge of the sale. *I wonder if I'll ever get back there; it's been two years.*

Bette's short tone matched her mother's. "I haveta share my room with *you!*"

Bernice's bland statement, "You girls are sisters now," did not alter twelve-year-old Bette's attitude of belligerency.

But that first Sunday things changed — Lynn met Joel Evans. He was playing his trumpet in the church youth group to lead the singing. The friendly girl sitting beside her was his sister Julie; she had the same brown eyes and dark shining hair. Lynn's loneliness melted in the warmth of her smile.

Someone sang "The Love of God" and Lynn couldn't keep the tears from dropping. *Home* was so far away. They sang choruses which lifted her spirit. Then Joel joined in a brass trio of "This World Is Not My Home." Lynn hummed the tune, the words filled her thoughts: *O Lord, you know, I have no friend like You. If heaven's not my home, then Lord, what will I do . . . .*

Their eyes met during that song and Joel came after the meeting to ask her name.

"Oh, yes, Bert Hale's daughter. He said you'd arrive Labor Day weekend. Welcome to Grace youth group. I see you've met my sister."

10

And Julie said, "Here's my pal, Sherry — you'll love her . . . ."

The rest of the conversation was garbled in the playback of the years. Certain scenes stood out: the first week of her senior year and Joel's attempt at reviving the Bible club at Howard High.

Some of the teachers showed contempt. The one in sociology started a discussion: "The Bible has no place in the school." But he was quick to preach his own religion of atheism.

That first week they had only a handful at club. Afterward they crossed the street to the crowded drugstore and gathered around the soda fountain.

Sherry wanted a ten-cent coke, and Julie said, "Make mine cherry, Sherry. Take this dollar — treat's on me. Lynn and I will find a table."

Someone shouted through the mob, "Come where the action is, Julie! Your brother is scooping up the news of the opening game."

They joined the boys at Joel's booth and someone yelled, "So who cares about Prince High? Let 'em trot out in their classy white duds!"

"Yeah! We'll mess 'em up."

"Come Friday night, we'll smear 'em at the mud bowl. The princeys'll eat dirt!"

Joel stopped scribbling in his notebook to smile at the girls. Lynn's heart leaped when he smiled.

A tall fellow in a maroon shirt swung down the aisle toward their table. Lynn glanced up. He leaned across the top of their booth to talk to Joel.

"Hey, Joel, got your pad? Here's a scoop for October's *Howard High Lights*. Craig Barr, our ace tackle, predicts a big year — says our team's out to win. Right, fellows?"

Whistles and laughter followed. The fellows packed around the tall one, draping arms over the top of the booths.

A broad-shouldered fellow in football sweater stood with feet wide apart, draining a coke. Lynn didn't like his satirical smile nor his cryptic comment: "Yeah! And put

11

this down in your little book, Joe. What we need to win this year are guys that can *kick* — not pray!"

The tall one's mouth sagged. "All *right*, Craig Barr — "

Craig shot them a knowing smirk, brushed an arm across his thick lips, and shuffled off muttering, "Him and his *Bible* club!"

The group scattered.

Sherry bristled like a bantam, her curly head bobbing around. "Ha! It takes real courage to head a Bible club in school, big mouth! I'll bet he's too chicken to even show up at our club!"

The tall one's laugh was contagious and the girls joined him.

"I'll visit your club," he said, looking down at Lynn intently. He lowered his tone. "Say! Will I see you at the opening game?"

"We have a party at our church every Friday night after the game."

The tall fellow stared. Then he exploded. "You call *that* school spirit? Why can't you guys join the crowd? You meet Fridays after school, right? Isn't that enough religion for one day?"

Joel smiled. "It isn't religion."

"Brother! I don't know what else you'd call it. Now I will visit your pray-in. This I gotta see!"

The tall one bent over Lynn. "Everybody comes to the dance in the gym after the game. Especially redheads. Why do you have to be so exclusive?"

"We're not," she said solemnly. "You're welcome to join us — "

His laughter shattered her words. Two girls sauntered up to their group. One was tall and dark, the other short with a mound of stiff bleached hair.

Julie got up and Lynn and Sherry followed, edging away from the strange girls and their sullen stares.

The tall boy was right behind Lynn. "I'll visit your club. Sorry if I sound dense, but this is something new on my beat. Say, you're from the south, aren't you? That southern drawl — "

Joel pushed the tall one along with his load of books and

the girls slipped through the mob to the street. Lynn felt her face burning.

Sherry grinned knowingly. "It's perfectly obvious — a guy fell in love with a beautiful redhead at first sight. And his name is Kurt Chase."

"Not the trombone!" Lynn swung around. "Was *that* Kurt Chase?"

"He's taller this year," Julie explained.

Sherry wailed, "If only I had half your looks, Lynn! You're the prettiest girl in school, and I'm not kidding." She patted Lynn's thick flip of hair which bounced up and down as she walked. "Lynn Hale, he had a lotta nerve calling you 'Red' when your hair is polished copper."

"Red gold," Julie remarked in her precise, reproving way.

"Oh, you girls!" Lynn's face flushed a brighter shade.

Sherry glanced over her shoulder. "That Craig! He keeps running around with that tough cycle crowd. He's no credit to Howard High, that's for sure." She crossed at the light and waved back. "See ya."

Lynn stopped under the bus sign. "Julie, I'm not sure about tonight. Thanks ever so much for coming home with me, though. You won't mind if Bernice doesn't let me go?"

"Lynn!" Julie's soft answer held a gentle reproach.

"Here comes the Germantown."

The bus was packed as usual. They stumbled down the aisle, clasping heavy books with one hand and a ceiling strap with the other.

"You have a long ride after you transfer, don't you, Lynn?"

"I'm used to it now. But when I first came from Virginia, it was a nightmare."

The girls changed buses, rode another mile, and got off at a large shopping center.

"Oh, Julie, I almost forgot! Bernice wants dinner rolls from Horn's. It'll only take a minute."

"Take your time, Lynn. I'm not in a hurry."

"But I'm late already!"

"You're always so nervous, Lynn. Relax!"

From the stores they walked rapidly along the avenue and mounted the steps to 36007. Lynn opened the door and

13

paused to adjust her load. The package of rolls dangled below her books.

Julie moved to one side to hold the screen.

A strident voice from within greeted them. "Lynn Hale! It's about time you got here! You know very well I can't be kept waiting Friday nights — or any other night! The table isn't set. I come home tired from my work. *You know that.* I expect you here the minute I get here! I can't be bothered with — where *are* you? Get in here!"

A neighbor opened her door to glance across the porches, and the girls scurried inside.

3

LYNN STUMBLED AND DROPPED her load. Julie knelt in the hall to help pick up the books. She murmured, "Don't worry."

The voice rasped on. "You never consider *me*, do you? I suppose you think it's child's play to teach music all afternoon! I come home, get the meal on, rush out to school affairs with your father all evening — oh! Who is this with you?" Bernice Hale rubbed a hand across her eyes as though trying to see and gave a short apologetic laugh. "I — well, I've had a rough day."

"Julie came over to help me work on a school project."

Julie took the cue. "Mrs. Hale, I was sure you wouldn't mind if I take Lynn home with me to spend the night. We have this float to design for the homecoming game. Joel and some boys from school said they'd help us tomorrow. But first, let us help you. May I set the table?"

"Lynn knows what to do. Yes, you may as well help. You find me at loose ends here, but you know how important my job is. And with my choir practice. Well! Two nights a week leading the First Street choir — besides the Grace youth groups. I was telling Bert only this morning that he would have to take over the youth choirs at Grace — I

14

simply have to draw the line somewhere." Bernice brushed a hand across her forehead. Her short hair frizzed upward. She shuffled down the hall in her thongs. Her jersey sheath dress made her look stout.

"Come upstairs and wash, Julie," Lynn whispered hoarsely.

In the upper hallway a large girl who looked like Bernice padded out in bare feet, licking a candy wrapper. She bulged in knit shirt and shorts.

"Hello, Bette," Julie said warmly.

"Hi." The girl's tone, like her pale eyes, lacked luster. She stared at Lynn. "Mom said for you to iron my pleated skirt the minute you got here. I gotta wear it tonight."

Lynn was breathless. "It won't take long, Julie. Here is your towel."

"I'm not worried, Lynn. Our dinner hour is always later on Fridays."

Lynn hurried to her room and deposited the load of books on her desk. Her twin bed was littered with Bette's books and papers.

"Bette — "

"Okay, *Okay.* Just leave my stuff alone."

"It doesn't look nice. I'm ashamed for Julie to see — "

"So *what?* Whatcha gonna *do* about it?" Bette threw herself face down across her bed and picked up a half-eaten apple. "It's *my* room!"

Lynn raced downstairs. Bernice yanked pans from the stove drawer and slammed lids around. "Can't find the dumb thing when I want it!" she sputtered. "What's the matter with you?" she hissed through set teeth. "You know better than to bring someone home with you — on Friday night of all nights in the week. Oh, here is your father! Bert, darling! How are you? You need a good meal. If it weren't for this capable daughter of yours, I would have had the meat loaf mixed and in the oven by this time. She is *so* helpful at times!"

Her note of sarcasm flooded Lynn with shame. She looked on helplessly as her father kissed Bernice, then glanced reproachfully at her. "What now?" he said lightly and picked up the evening paper.

15

"Oh, hello, Julie," she heard him say in the hall. "We'll have to get started this fall with our music, won't we? Pastor says we should keep the orchestra going in Sunday evening service."

Bernice cornered Lynn in the kitchen and snapped in an undertone, "I was counting on you to be here while I go to that school open house with Bert. Bette will be all alone here with those girls. Someone will have to help with her pizza party tonight."

"Bette is nearly thirteen now." Lynn was trembling.

"Unwilling to help your family! I always said your mother spoiled you! You cause me all kinds of trouble with your selfishness, girl. Look at me!"

Lynn looked up. As usual, her stepmother's face and neck were red. Lynn avoided the stinging accusation in her eyes.

Lynn's throat tightened. "I'll stay," she whispered hoarsely.

Later that evening while she was ironing in the basement, Bette called down, "Lynn! Phone!"

The girls' party was going strong. Joel said, "I can't hear you, Lynn. What's going on?"

"I can hardly hear you either. Bette and some girls are having a pizza party."

"And you'll have the whole kitchen to clean up, won't you? Lynn, I hope you can get away by two tomorrow for the committee meeting. Tell you what. I'll call Bernice about noon and suggest that since I am out your way — my barber shop is sort of in that direction — I could drop by and pick you up."

Lynn laughed with him. His camaraderie scattered the gloom of her lonely evening. They discussed the approaching football season.

"Had to air the old band uniform. Mother had it stored in English lavender! And say! Kurt Chase wanted to know more about you — I gave him a lift today. Lives in an apartment hotel off the parkway. His dad is the architect, Chase — quite a big wheel in town.

"Anyway, Kurt was trying to figure out why you girls

16

are different from the ones he knows. You in particular. Y'know, Lynn, I think he'll visit our club. You might even get him to come with us Saturday night to the rally."

"Why don't you ask him?" she teased.

Joel laughed. "I did. More than once. He doesn't get it — you know — that crowd can't understand us. 'Two different worlds,' he said. And of course he's right."

"Joel, I'm awfully sorry but —"

"I know." She could almost see his dark eyes spark. "You have a lot of work to get done. Okay, Lynn, see you tomorrow."

The kindness in his tone always shook her. How she had looked forward to an evening at the Evans home. She brushed a sudden mist from her eyelashes and sped downstairs.

As usual the ironing basket was stacked high. Bette was supposed to do the flatwork, but one thing or another kept her from her part of the ironing.

The phone rang upstairs and again Bette yelled down, "Lynn!" in an exasperated scream.

Lynn hurried to answer.

The strong voice was unmistakable. "Hi, Lynn. Kurt Chase. Remember — this afternoon?"

"Yes?"

"I can't get you off my mind — not that I've tried. That southern drawl! Those amber —"

"Kurt, I'm sorry but —"

"You mean you're going steady?"

"No, not exactly. But —"

"Then you can go out with me."

"No, I can't."

"C'mon, now, ya gotta start livin'! Just because you've been brought up in a convent doesn't mean you can't have fun and find out about life. Give me one good reason for not going out with me next Friday night!"

"I would rather go with the group. Why don't you come with us? Joel Evans usually takes me to the party after the game. That is, he takes a group of us girls — his sis and friends. You are more than welcome to ride with us and —"

"That Pauline Porter in your crowd? Ha! She cheats

17

just like the rest, and old dame Diddenheimer casts her sights on that Bible-packin' prude and gives her straight A's. Sorry, that's not your fault. Look, Lynn, give me a break!"

"Thanks for asking me, Kurt, but I really have a load of work tonight, so — "

"Homework? What subjects? I can be all kinds of help — a shark at math."

"That's all done."

"Tell ya, I'll give you moral support . . . I'll bring my books over and study."

"Good-by, Kurt. I'll see you at school Monday. I have a big ironing to do."

"It's not good-by. See ya *tomorrow*, Lynn!"

Lynn replaced the receiver, a smile tugging at her mouth. What a guy! Did he know about their committee meeting at Joel's?

4

WHEN JULIE ARRIVED HOME Friday evening, she found her family preparing for late dinner. Mrs. Evans lighted yellow candles. A centerpiece of yellow and orchid fall flowers shed fragrance in the house. Joel stood at the kitchen sink thawing ice cube trays, whistling in tune with the stereo.

Julie carried salad plates into the dining room. Through the picture window she saw the blue spruce trees darkening in the purple dusk.

Mr. Evans took his place at the head of the table. Joel held his sister's chair and mumbled in her ear, "Cinderella again?"

She nodded. Their father prayed. Then he looked at his daughter. "Isn't Lynn supposed to be here tonight, honey?"

"Yes — " Julie sighed.

"Mother — " Julie paused once more. "It's difficult to express in words, but I think there is something deeper than mere family friction going on over there."

Mrs. Evans remained placid. "I think Bernice rides herd at home with more force because she is accustomed to school routine. You must remember," Mrs. Evans continued, "the Hales are a gifted couple. Bert is top orchestra and band leader in the city schools, and Bernice is extremely gifted. Besides her choir directing, she teaches a class of women in Sunday school. I've talked with Bernice and she seems quite pleasant."

"She rides on just one of the herd — Lynn!" Joel observed wryly.

Mr. Evans laughed. "I'd say we had better change the subject. Mother, these biscuits are delicious."

After dinner Joel looked at his sister and said lightly, "Guess I'll call Lynn."

His mother paused in the doorway. "I want you to keep something in mind, son. This friendship is fine for your high school days, but you are graduating this January. You have several more years of college, and your father and I are hoping you will meet a dedicated and talented young lady whose background is similar to yours.

"You have much to consider in the selection of a wife. She will be your partner for life. And, as I have often said, you must steel yourself to look at each friend objectively. Sometimes it is easy to mistake pity or admiration for love."

Her composure nettled him. Joel tapped fingers on the stereo.

Julie sensed her brother's frustration. She knew he cared about Lynn, perhaps more than she or her parents knew. What did her mother mean about *background similar to?* Wealth, prestige, or what? Everyone liked Bert Hale and his daughter, Lynn.

When the Hales first arrived in the area, her mother had remarked that something was wrong with that pretty, red-headed girl. *All that is wrong with Lynn is her unhappy home life.* Why couldn't Mother and Dad see through such people as Bernice? *If they knew Lynn as Joel and I do, they wouldn't want him to look at another girl!*

As Lynn ran out to meet Joel the next afternoon, she

felt as light and free as the tumbling clouds in the aqua sky. Her smile brought an answering light in his eyes, but his tone lacked its usual lilt.

"Guess who's joining our meeting!"

"Kurt Chase?"

"How did you guess? Did he call you?"

"He wanted to come over last night. I invited him to the party next Friday."

"He isn't interested in church, Lynn. It's you he wants to know. Of course — if he goes along — " Joel reached for her hand.

"Don't worry about that." She moved closer to him. "We should start praying that he will meet Christ and start living. That crowd doesn't know what life *is*. And they think *we're* the dumb ones."

"That's what I like about you, Lynn. You're solid gold. Not many girls in our group would look at it that way. Kurt has dough — owns his own wheels or borrows his dad's foreign jobs — he's popular and all the girls are crazy about him."

"Well, I'm not! I don't even want to talk about him. What's Julie doing?"

"Baking a cake to serve at committee."

They glided from busy streets to the curving boulevard and Joel slowed the car to a crawl. "Lynn, I received admission papers from the Bible college in New York, but I'm not excited over the prospects. I wanted to major in journalism, but the folks want me to have at least one year of Bible training before I go to State. So it looks as though I'll be leaving in January." He pressed her hand gently.

As they turned into Evans' circular drive, their eyes met. Joel's sober gaze chilled her. Shakily she stepped from the car. As they crossed the lawn to the patio, she tried to shake the sadness. Their wonderful years of high school were coming to an end. She couldn't imagine Philadelphia without Joel.

Julie called from the kitchen. Lynn found her at the sink, washing the electric beater. "It'll just take a sec to frost this cake, Lynn." Julie handed her a towel and the wet beater. "Sherry will soon be here — and of course Pauline.

20

Someone named Gil Stone is on the committee too, and I suppose Joel told you that Kurt wants to show us some fantastic plan for a float. But guess who he's dragging along! That wild Craig Barr!"

Lynn gasped. "Why does *he* have to come?"

"He's probably Kurt's buddy. They run around with those two girls we saw in the drugstore Friday. That short blond is Kurt's current craze."

Car wheels crackled on gravel. They heard Sherry's squeal for help and ran out with Joel. They found her sliding a huge cardboard box from the rear door of a station wagon. She grinned impishly, her freckled little nose wrinkling.

Pauline Porter slowly climbed from the car and slouched to the scene of action. Her unkept hair hung in her eyes; she shook her head in vain attempts at clearing her vision.

Lynn's smile faded. Pauline's attitude always dampened their spirits. As usual, her blouse needed pressing and her skirt looked as though it had never been cleaned. A Bible lay on top of her books.

"Here, Pauline, you take this box and Julie — "

"Let Lynn take it. I'm beat!" Pauline sagged against the car door.

Sherry cracked, "Yeah! Her backbone isn't stiff enough to handle this job."

Pauline stiffened and she picked up a smaller box, stomped down to the rec room, and slapped her books on a table.

A car spun in the drive. Joel took the steps three at a time and they heard his welcome. "Kurt! Craig! And Gil! Come in. We're all down here."

Pauline stood stiffly with hands on hips. As Craig swept by, she snapped, "I'm not interested in a hippie hangout, Joel Evans! I thought this was to be a committee meeting!"

Craig stopped short. "Meaning *what?*" he asked.

Pauline blazed in his face. "You should know!"

Lynn tensed. Didn't Pauline know better than to rile a fellow like Craig Barr?

Craig flung a contemptuous glance and slammed boxes to the floor. "You're crazy! You don't even know what a hippie *is!* Now Kurt could give — "

Kurt whirled and slapped Craig hard on the back. "Here,

21

man! I want you to meet some *real* Christians. You too, Gil — a Jew should learn the difference. There are lemons in every bunch, and I mean sour — ugh! But here's Julie Evans, Joel's sis. She's a peach. And these over here — Lynn and Sherry!"

Pauline grabbed her sweater and books and bounded for the stairs. Joel followed. "I'll drive you home, Pauline, if you can't stay."

"*If* I can't stay? Do you *expect* me to stay? You, Joel Evans, the president of our youth group — and this is the company you keep!"

Craig muttered an oath. They heard Joel's call, "All right, then, if that's the way you feel about it."

Kurt looked thoughtfully at Julie. "Told your brother I'd show you a gimmick with moving parts for your float.

"Hey, Joe! Come down. You gotta hear this. My brother in New York won an award in engineering at his university — and had the best float in the homecoming. That was last year, and we could make a copy of it, with changes here and there — old Uncle Scrooge's moneymaking machine. He had big figures of Scrooge and the little ducks, and the moneymachine had wires and stuff sticking out. It was great. Worked by a piston which pushed out silver and gold cardboard coins onto a conveyor belt. They had a crooked smokestack belching black smoke — operated it by a lever inside the works. Man, it was a neat layout.

"The guys from Hal's frat waltzed along the street beside the float dressed as clowns, tossing candy kisses to the kids. Made a big hit. The judges liked their contact with the crowd. Topped all other contestants. Believe me, they had fancy floats by the furlong."

"By the *what?*"

"Bible lingo. Don't you ever read the world's best seller, Craig, old man?"

Craig swore and Joel said quickly, "Doesn't sound like it. You know, Craig, that old Book has power. It changes lives."

Gil's head jerked up.

Craig rolled his eyes. "Yipe! You're a sky pilot if I ever saw one. I get the creeps when anyone talks religion. Let me outa here!"

22

Kurt towered over him. He grasped Craig's sweater in a tight grip and pulled his face close. "You're stayin' with me, see?"

"Okay, Okay, just don't give me any of that religion stuff! When you're dead, you're dead, and nobody's gonna tell me different."

Joel helped Gil with a paint can. He said under his breath, "So when you die, Craig, we'll just toss you in the city dump along with the garbage, like a dead dog. No funeral — if you're worth no more than an animal."

Craig scratched his head and grinned at the girls.

Sherry laughed. "Pretty good, Joel."

Kurt opened a folding chair and sat in it backwards, leaning elbows on top. "I see your point there, Joe. Y'know, I do feel higher than an animal at that."

"Sure. Dogs don't have souls." Joel and Gil were stirring paint. Craig paced around the tables nervously.

"Finally Gil said, "So?"

Joel cut a piece of cardboard with a knife. "Dogs have something in common with us; they have bodies. Right? They get injured and feel pain as we do; they are conscious of the world around them."

"So?" Gil repeated.

"So men are like animals in that respect. Dogs are also like us in being conscious of self: when you scold your dog he whines and looks sorrowful. When you praise him, he shows his joy by wagging his tail. Right?"

"Uh-huh." Kurt rocked on his chair.

"One thing your dog lacks, and that is a soul or God-consciousness. An animal is not created with this third dimension. Did you ever see a dog bow in prayer? Yet every man — even the ignorant savage — is conscious of a higher power. Some poor souls even stretch their bodies on beds of spikes trying to earn their way to some sort of paradise by doing penance to some higher power. Others walk on their knees until they are torn and bleeding.

"That's the reason we send missionaries to tell them the Gospel — the good news that God sent His only begotten Son to suffer *for* them and to pay the price for their sins, His own life's blood."

23

"A good philosophy." Kurt rubbed his chin thoughtfully. "Not a philosophy, Kurt. God's Word."

"Broth—er!" Craig kicked a pile of cardboard from underfoot and stood with feet wide apart. His thick lips twisted in a cynical grin. Then he laughed boisterously, slapping his hands together. "Give me some of that paint, girls. I didn't come over here to get converted!"

Gil smiled. "So, why get excited? To me, Joel, this is interesting. I mean — to hear another religious viewpoint. It's educational. However, if you don't mind my saying so, we are all trying to get to the same place. We Jews do not believe God *had* a Son. Any person who lives right, is a good neighbor, as your Christian Bible teaches, is on the right track. After all — "

"What difference does it make?" Kurt settled back in his chair, yawned, stretched both arms, and looked dreamily at Lynn. "Plenty of time to meditate when I'm too old for dancing and song. Oh, you beautiful doll . . ."

5

JOEL WAS ENTHUSIASTIC. "Kurt! You've got a voice!"

Lynn's face burned, but she had to speak. "If you'd like to see what God can do with a voice like yours, Kurt, go with us to the youth rally tonight. The former opera star, Jerrold Mills, is going to sing."

"What's with him? Wasn't he good enough to stay in show biz?" Craig's jaw dropped.

"He was so good he got promoted, Craig," Joel said quietly. "Now he not only delights people with his singing, but he can also show them the way of real peace — the way to God. He is using his talent for the Lord."

Kurt looked at them soberly. Craig padded around the table trying to swallow his unfavorable comments about

God, but they spilled over in low grumbles. "Huh!" he spouted. "Wasn't he already using his ability to make people feel better? Wasn't he making people happy in show biz? What more could he do for — for *God?*" He pulled a folding chair from the wall and sat in it backwards beside Kurt.

Joel answered, "As long as we stay apart from God — living merely for ourselves and this world — *nothing* we do can please God. But in the Spirit — "

"There ya go again!" Craig bounded to his feet and crossed the room in restless strides. "Talkin' about spirits! It's spooky! You guys live in a different world. Whatcha *get* out of being so — such — "

"Squares? Octagons?" Sherry sputtered.

"Well, since ya put it that way!" Craig wheeled to face Joel. "You're not with it, man!"

Lynn caught a wink from Sherry. The girls stopped working and stared when Sherry began to snap her fingers above her head and hum a catchy little tune they had heard in the school assembly.

In a sultry voice she sang, "So *what?* Who *cares!*" until they recognized Marla West's throaty wail. Sherry imitated her number to perfection, even the facial expressions.

Kurt exploded in laughter. "Marla! How *about* that, Craig?"

Craig's mouth sagged.

Sherry kept up the song, imitating Marla's bored indifference, until the girls shrieked with laughter. Sherry ended in a whirl around the ping-pong table and called out to Craig, "That's the only spirit *you* guys know!"

"Okay, *Okay*," Craig grinned at her. "I give. Say, Kurt, I gotta cut out. Jodi's waiting for me to pick her up. Gonna blow to N'York for the weekend."

The girls exchanged glances.

Kurt gazed dreamily at Lynn. "Who knows? Maybe these ethereal maids will take me into their exclusive club. A pass to paradise."

Craig looked disgusted. "Just to put the record straight — about Jodi and me. She has an aunt in the city, top of Central Park, where she stays — "

"Ha! Ha! And ha!" Kurt sneered.

Joel yelled, "Cut! Let's get to work!"

Kurt wheeled to attention. "Now about this float. How does Uncle Scrooge's moneymaking machine sound to you guys?"

Sherry shrieked with satisfying enthusiasm. "It's the greatest, Kurt!"

He beamed in appreciation.

It seemed they had just started trying to revise their work plans when Mrs. Evans came down with a tray of soda and pretzels. Julie dropped her stencils. "I'll rustle up cake and sandwiches. Help me, girls?"

Craig cocked his head at the soft drinks. "Might have known — no bar in a sky pilot's basement. Well, here's where Barr heads for some hooch. Bye, Joe. Gotta scram."

Lynn was surprised when Kurt paid no attention to him, nonchalantly picked up a tray and loaded it with pretzels.

Joel walked outside with Craig but came right back. "Said he'd catch the bus."

"Sure," Kurt said easily. "Fish outa water. Me — I'm beginning to dig paradise." He grinned at the girls.

"Speaking of paradise," Sherry remarked later upstairs, "this is the preview, Julie. The rest of us ordinary mortals live in more conventional style: one bath to a family, inch of balcony overlooking paved alley, no lawn or garden. It's beautiful, kid, but I wouldn't trade our small row house for all the mansions from here to the west coast. We have wonderful neighbors and our little place is home sweet home.

"Of course, with my dad unconcerned about spiritual things, it has been hard on Mom and the whole family. You are the ideal family in the church, Julie. 'Given to hospitality, apt to teach . . .' everything we studied about last Sunday."

"Which reminds me." Julie perched on a pink velvet bench at her dressing table. "Sunday school promotion is in October, and I hope we get Miss Lindy. I heard she was asked to help out in senior high this fall."

"Oh, you'll love Miss Lindy!" Sherry's freckled face beamed. "Lynnie, have you ever had her — Miss Melinda Mapes?"

"No. Is she the tiny white-haired lady? Little, thin, and

26

fragile looking? Yes, I've noticed her because she has such twinkling black eyes. She is so friendly and sparkling."

"That describes her all right. And you should see her house! A Betsy Ross replica set right on the brick sidewalk in a block of ancient red-brick houses. Cute little window boxes full of petunias all summer."

A car motor raced.

Julie yelped, "Oh, oh! We'd better scram."

The girls raced downstairs and outside.

Kurt leaped from the front seat, but Joel called out, "Stay here! Three in front and three in the rear. They're slim as sardines."

Kurt sniffed. "Sure don't smell like 'em. Get a load of that perfumed bouquet. Ah, paradise!" He threw his arm over the seat behind Gil and kept watching the girls. "I'm sitting with them after we stop by Stone's. No fun going stag to a youth rally."

Joel laughed. "Lynn can sit up here between us and Gil can take the back."

Julie whispered, "I didn't know Gil was going with us. Isn't he fascinating?"

Sherry nodded. "Sure is handsome. And a nice guy!" She raised her voice. "Look at *these* houses! Aren't they gorgeous? All in soft gray stone. Which house do the Stones — ?"

"The corner one. Right here, Joel," Gil directed. "And you can pull into the drive. I'll only be a minute."

Kurt grinned at the girls. "Watch this. I don't take to the Yids. At least, my father doesn't. But the Stones are different. That's them coming out to meet us. Friendliest folks you'll ever find. And can she ever cook! Wow! Gourmet specials."

Sherry said, "She looks motherly — short and chubby — and her face is sweet."

Julie noticed Mr. Stone. "He's even shorter than she."

"But he's thin. What a fragile looking man."

Lynn warmed to Gil's grandparents even while they walked to the car.

"What a good time you are having already!" Mrs. Stone's rippling laugh greeted each one.

Mr. Stone's accent also revealed his nationality. Lynn was fascinated and strangely moved by their gracious manner. What a unique couple.

Mr. Stone's words came more slowly than his wife's. His refined speech was reminiscent of an old world culture. "We appreciate this — asking our grandson to be with you. All these years we are raising him since his mother died — may she rest in peace — and we are bringing up Gilbert from Bar Mitzvah until now, and only once already is a Christian saying, 'We like your company.'"

Joel smiled back as he started the motor. "That is because there are few *real* Christians in the world, Mr. Stone. Our pastor has begun a series of messages on the tabernacle in the Old Testament — the old covenant God made with Israel compared with the new. You know about the tabernacle in the wilderness? In the first books of the Bible?"

"I tell you," Mr. Stone said, "we don't know too much about the Bible. We have learned rabbis who study these things."

"We'd love to take you with us some Sunday to hear our pastor, Mrs. Stone," Julie invited.

The Jewish lady smiled and reached across Lynn to pat Julie's arm. "You are a darling. But all day Sammy is working hard at the office. We usually sleep late Sunday mornings. We have a late coffee, read the papers, and sometimes we are taking a little ride."

Mr. Stone's soft voice added, "We could have our dinner earlier in the afternoon some Sunday, Sarah. And you young people could be eating with us. What you think?"

Mrs. Stone beamed and took her husband's arm. "Of course, Sammy. And thank you, Joel, for asking Gil to be going with you. I hope it will do him good." She chuckled and waved at the girls.

Kurt waved Lynn into the front seat as Gil swung down the drive, adjusting his coat collar. Joel called out, "Gil! You don't have to wear a tie. That isn't a — "

Gil shrugged and opened the rear door. "So, I should waste your time changing again? Let's go. We're late already from stopping on my account."

"It won't take long to pick up burgers and fries." Joel waved at the Stones and backed to the street.

"Treat's on me next time," Kurt mumbled in Lynn's ear.

"Gil!" The girls were all talking at once. Julie's voice came through. "Gil, your grandparents are such dear people. It seems as though I have known them for a long time."

Gil nodded vigorously. "Thank you. Thank you, girls. Yes, you'll never meet better people in this world — and they mean the whole world to me."

Lynn moved closer to Joel as they skimmed down the avenue toward Roosevelt Boulevard. It was good to be with her friends, away from the unrest in her father's house. She hummed, and Kurt bent his head to catch the tune.

Gil said, "I'm curious. Why do you have a Bible club in school? We Jews have our studies in the synagogue."

"I'm curious too, or you wouldn't find me sitting here riding to *church* on a *Saturday* night!" Kurt shot Gil a wry smile.

Julie laughed. "They have all kinds of clubs in school. Why not? You'd have to attend one, Gil, to see for yourself."

"I see. So you have a study like mine for Bar Mitzvah maybe. I went to Hebrew school two afternoons a week until I was thirteen."

"How could you stand it?" Kurt yelped. "I don't mind a little discussion about religion. But to have it crammed down like breakfast cereal — ugh!"

"I don't go for 'religion' either, Kurt." Joel's dark eyes flashed. "You'll find this rally something different."

When they took seats in the auditorium, Sherry nudged the girls. "They're supposed to have a funny skit tonight. That scream of a team from East Church."

Julie whispered across Lynn, "Kurt should enjoy that."

Kurt overheard and leaned from his seat beside Joel. "No fun — I'm missing all they're saying, Joe. I'm sitting between Lynn and Sherry. Mind?"

Lynn opened her mouth but said nothing as Gil, Joel, and Julie moved over to let Kurt in. He immediately took Sherry's hand on one side and Lynn's on the other, heaved a big sigh, and hummed a tune.

6

THE GIRLS COULDN'T KEEP their faces straight. Kurt looked solemn. "No nicer girls in Howard. I'm in the right groove at last." He released Sherry's hand and held Lynn's but a second longer, then turned in his seat to survey the crowd. "Hmm. Thousands upon hundreds. How many does this place seat, anyway? How many bus loads and cars come here, I'd like to know?

"Hey, Gil! This crowd beats any youth meeting I've ever seen at our church. We can't even get a third this many when we hire a dance combo. And this crowd hasn't come to dance!"

Gil leaned over Joel. "I know what you mean. Our temple is full only on high holidays. I must say, Joel, I am quite impressed."

Stage curtains rose, lights dimmed, and the spotlight centered on three fellows sitting around a mike at a long table, scripts in hand. A fourth stood by a record player which spouted jazz. He turned down the volume and spoke into a tall microphone.

"This is your favorite station 'Where M I' with news every other hour as soon as it is stale. And now we'll enjoy 'Gaslight Serenade.'" He flicked the record player with one finger and a trombone blared for only thirty seconds, diminishing to a low wail when the announcer barked, "And now a word from our sponsor."

Two fellows from the table took the mike. "Are you smoking less and enjoying it more? Then you'll want to hear from a satisfied customer. Cyrus, I understand you have been inhaling our product, *Weedyburros,* a year this very day. Step right up to the mike and tell us all about it.

30

Here he is, folks, Cyrus Pratt from Pottsdown, veteran sucker of *Weedyburros*."

The audience broke into laughter as Cyrus started a spasmodic coughing spell. Grasping the mike with one hand, his tall, lean frame doubled as he clutched his chest, coughed, and tried to sputter a few words over the mike. The kids in the hall laughed so long that he gave up and staggered back to his place at the table.

When the room quieted a little, the announcer said, "Our coughing friend reminds me of a mummy. That's an Egyptian who had a long coffin' spell! And now we interrupt this commercial to bring you a special program, the Jeep Boys."

The three fellows put their heads together and harmonized.

"They're good singers," Kurt whispered in Lynn's ear.

The thin one's strong baritone surprised everyone.

Kurt leaned across Lynn so Julie could hear. "He's a singer as well as a comedian. Y'know, these kids are good!"

While another curtain rose, revealing a row of musicians and a grand piano, the broadcasting group moved offstage. The baritone stayed at the tall mike.

Lynn whispered, "He's Wes Marks, one of the youth leaders. He helps kids get these Bible clubs organized in the schools, and he usually leads the singing at the big rallies here."

A low whistle from Kurt accompanied the applause when a tall girl walked on stage to the piano. Lynn nudged Julie. Each read the other's thoughts. Sherry voiced her opinion, "Am I ever glad it's Angie tonight!"

Lynn whispered, "And is she ever stunning in that dress!"

Wes waved a song book. "Turn to page eight, please. And let's all stand."

Lynn knew Kurt would appreciate the orchestra. At the leader's signal thousands of young voices rang to the joyous lilt of "He Lives."

Kurt kept looking down at Lynn. She sensed his wonder at the lively music. The hall reverberated to the rising crescendo of "He lives, He lives, Christ Jesus lives today."

When they sat down, Kurt said under his breath, "And

here I was thinking your rally would be dead like my church. Man! I've never heard such singing. Maybe I *will* come — "

He stopped as three attractive girls approached the mike. Sherry whispered, "The Joy Trio of radio and TV."

"Yeah?" he muttered.

Lynn was excited. The girls were well-known in Christian music circles; their harmonizing of gospel songs was thrilling. When each gave a personal word on her commitment to Christ, Lynn prayed that something might get through to Kurt.

When they had finished, Wes said, "And now we have that special treat promised you for this evening. The singer of former opera fame — the one and only — Jerrold Mills!"

The applause stampeded as a tall and powerfully built man strode on stage.

Gil said, "I saw him in New York once in *Aida*." Then he settled back to listen.

Mills' strong voice began, "The Joy Trio's last song carried me back to the night of my decision for Christ. I was ill with a throat infection in a hotel room in Detroit and was forced to cancel my engagement.

"We were playing *Madame Butterfly* on a tour across country. I was sick in body; I was tired in mind; and I was secretly bored with the crowd who gushed over us after each performance at the parties held in our honor. I was thinking — is this all there is to life — playing the same part night after night, repeating performances for months on end — all for the applause of society? What is life all about?

"I was dissatisfied with my life. Something was missing. And that night when I tuned in to an evangelistic program, I found that it wasn't *something* I was missing — it was *Someone!*

"A former opera star was singing that night. The testimony he gave was the same as I have just told you. His experience was mine. And he declared that he had found the answer to life in the person of Jesus Christ, the Messiah, the only begotten Son of God. This same Jesus is the One I declare unto you tonight."

Jerrold Mills nodded to the musicians and stepped back from the mike. His voice thrilled the audience.

> There's a new song in my heart
> Since the Savior set me free;
> There's a new song in my heart —
> 'Tis a heav'nly harmony!
> All my sins are washed away
> In the blood of Calvary;
> Oh what peace and joy
> Nothing can destroy —
> There's a new song in my heart!*

Mills lifted his Bible. "The atoning blood of the Lamb is evident from the first book, Genesis, right through to Revelation where we last see the Lamb of God — not as the meek and lowly servant who walked this earth, but as King of kings and Lord of lords.

"Turn to the first chapter of John, verses eleven and twelve. 'He came unto his own, and his own received him not. But as many as received him, to them gave he power to become the sons of God, even to them that believe on his name.' This may surprise you, but I am a Jew who has accepted Jesus as the Messiah and Redeemer of Israel and my own personal Saviour."

Lynn and Julie glanced over to see Gil's reaction. He sat forward tensely, clenching his hands. Joel whispered, "This is a surprise to me, Gil. I didn't know he was Jewish."

Gil scowled. "He isn't. He's a traitor to his race. He is no longer a Jew!"

7

LYNN CAUGHT THE BUS Monday morning and met Sherry when she got off to transfer.

Sherry's first words echoed Lynn's thoughts. "Was I

*© 1955 by Singspiration, Inc. All rights reserved. Used by permission.

shook up when they didn't show!" She climbed the steps and the bus lurched forward.

Lynn said, "Guess Kurt thought Saturday night was enough for one week."

"Yeah! I didn't really *think* he'd get Craig and those two girls to come." Sherry giggled. "Wasn't the music tops? Kurt kept saying, 'This is good! It's really good.' "

"And Mills' testimony was meant for Kurt. Even Gil admired his singing. But wasn't that a surprise about his being Jewish?"

Sherry nodded. "Anyway, our club is really swinging this year. If only Kurt can influence some of those kids to come!"

A mound of hair alerted Lynn. "That short blond up there. Isn't that Carla, the one Kurt goes with?"

"Sure is. Let's ask her, shall we?"

When the bus stopped at the corner of Howard, Sherry edged through the crowd and called, "Carla, wait!"

The girl's lazy insolence reminded Lynn of Bette. Carla shuffled over to them, chewing gum and peering at them from behind long shreds of coarse, bleached hair. She stared at Sherry.

Sherry gulped and looked up at Lynn with a thin smile. Lynn said, "We understood from Kurt that some of you might visit our church last night."

Carla shook hair from her eyes and laughed. They were on the school steps when she was finally able to answer: "That's funny! If you knew where we were last night!" She swore. Then she sobered. "He must have been kidding you guys. Kurt picked me up early Sunday morning and we drove up to N'York to meet Craig and Jodi. Did we ever have a blast! Did we ever!" She gave a shriek as she saw Jodi.

The tall girl tossed her head, fanning glossy black hair over her shoulders. Puffy, dark rings outlined her eyes. She yawned, surveying Carla from behind her screen of false lashes. "What's with you, jitterbug?"

This seemed to send Carla into a deeper spasm. Lynn and Sherry eased away, but Carla's high-pitched voice followed them. "*Church*, Jodi! Church — last night — just listen to this!"

34

The girls didn't wait to listen. They cut for classes as fast as they could. Lynn dreaded running into Kurt at band practice.

Joel was seated in the brass section, tuning his trumpet. Lynn returned his smile as she assembled her clarinet. When a large hand touched her shoulder, she looked up to see Kurt's wide, hazel eyes searching hers.

The shot of Carla's mockery produced a reaction and she shook loose. "Stop it!" She scowled and Kurt backed away.

A glance at his face showed her that Kurt was sober, but he looked as though he hadn't slept for a week. It flashed through her mind that Carla's view of Sunday was not necessarily his. Her face flamed and she stammered, "I'm sorry, Kurt, but you startled me."

Instantly he was at her side, a wide grin on his face. "It's me, that's who. Oh, oh! Cheese it! Here comes Smitty with his baton. Whack, whack, whack! Everything to him is four-four time! Man! Do I wish we had your dad for director. I've heard he's got real rhythm over there at South. Well, carry on, redhead. You're the — "

The band leader snapped, "Kurt Chase! In your place *if you please!*"

Kurt loped back to the trombone section muttering, "I please, sir. Ah yes, I please."

Lynn smiled through the hour. Kurt had personality plus. *But how can I shake him? What will Joel think?*

The girls met her at the lockers before lunch. Sherry whispered to Julie, "Is Pauline ever mad at *you!* She's been telling people tales about last Saturday."

Julie smiled. "As Mother says, 'consider the source.' I'm not the least perturbed."

Lynn wondered at Julie's command of the situation. Would Julie remain as calm if her mother was Bernice? How would Julie react to a person like Pauline Porter if she had to live with her? Was it possible to keep cool under constant pressure?

Pauline deliberately stalked past them, ignoring the girls. She took her place at the end of their table and began her usual noisy attack on a bulging lunch sack.

35

Julie called softly, "Hi, Pauline. Coming to help us work on the float after school?"

Pauline shook her head violently and glared at them. "You can't tell me *we're* supposed to waste *our* time with a bunch of hoodlums!"

Sherry snapped, "It wasn't wasted by us Saturday afternoon. Joel got Kurt Chase to go with us to the rally downtown. I'd say — "

Pauline snorted, "*I'd* say he wasn't interested in the youth rally. I can guarantee that!" She eyed Lynn with scorn.

Sherry crunched potato chips and grinned. "Why do you always carry a chip — what's eating you? As Pastor said last night, 'It's not so much what you *eat* that makes you upset; it's what's eating *you!*'"

"You make me sick!" Pauline pushed back her chair and stalked out.

The bell rang and the girls scrambled for the doors. In the crowd they met Jodi and Carla.

Jodi stared at them and said coolly, "Kurt says we should have a sit-in Friday at your club. What d'ya do?"

Julie smiled. "Ask Kurt about the rally. Our programs are similar. Come and see."

Jodi shrugged. "Might make it."

Lynn caught a glimpse of Carla's face before she moved around the corner. She was looking up at her friend in amazement.

The girls reported to Joel after school.

"Great! Just great! And Dr. Winkelman is coming. Remember, Julie? He'll stay at our house during the week's meetings at church, and I'm sure we can get him to speak to the kids at club."

Sherry squealed. "Boy! That *is* great! Doctor of science who believes the Bible to address the daughter of a doctor who doesn't! Lionel Lambert will not approve Jodi's sit-in with *us*, I'm afraid."

Joel laughed. Lynn felt his enthusiasm, but knew something had happened between them. She had a strange sensation of detachment from him. Since their conversation about his going away to college, he had been friendly, but the deep feeling they shared was not coming to the surface.

He seemed to avoid her. Of course he was terrifically busy. What could she expect?

But I could expect that with a boy like Joel — I could count on him. He does care. That wonderful spring day in the park he asked me to wait for him. He knew I was the girl he wanted to marry. We both knew. But things aren't the same. He is different somehow.

What had changed his attitude toward her? Lynn was still wondering Wednesday after school while they worked on the float. Joel, as committee chairman, had collected a gang of helpers outside the gym.

Sherry sighed audibly and attached another paper carnation to the chicken wire. "Where do all these extras come from? Our funds ran out after the first committee meet at your house, Julie."

"No mystery at all. Kurt was there and he's been on this project ever since. Money seems to be no problem. He's been running in and out of our house like a squirrel these days."

Jodi and Carla sauntered up, books in arms.

Sherry stretched to rest her arms, then sat on the ground to stuff the lower wires. "We were just saying that Kurt was the engineer of this float."

Carla stared at her. "Yeah, Kurt hasn't called me all week. Wasn't for this stupid old parade — "

Jodi looked on, interest replacing her bored expression. "Looks like fun. Need some help? We'll stay. Got my new car outside. Dad's birthday present to me. You'll all have to ride with me."

Sherry shoved a pack of paper napkins at them. "I could go for that, Jodi. Thanks. Help yourselves. The more help the better! I've got to get home sometime tonight and I've already missed my bus."

"Said I'd take you!" Jodi tossed her books to one side and got down on her knees.

Joel moved down the lines, inspecting, and stopped at their end of the wire frame. "Good for you, Jodi. Thanks for your help. And Carla! Great!" He yelled, "We're about ready to assemble the parts on the truck. Where's Kurt?"

A boy shouted from the doorway, "He's inside. I'll get him."

Joel called, "Now, everyone be ready to give him a big yell in thanks for — "

He was drowned out by screams and shrill whistles as Kurt bounded through the double doors.

Kurt looked pleased but his ears were red. Quick to catch his cue, he leaped to the back of the truck. "Now, gang, we want this float to be a big success. Joel Evans and his committee have worked night and day to put *Howard* on the sports map of our state. We want him to be able to scribble in his editorial column: '*Howard* takes first prize for the best float in Philly.' How about that?"

The air echoed with whistles and shouts for victory. Jodi screamed until her neck veins stood out. Sherry jumped up and down yelling, but a glance at Carla's impassive face froze her. What an utter lack of response!

"Kurt's sure gone!" was Carla's cold comment. Her eyes grazed Lynn with disgust.

Julie caught the inference. "Well, Carla, what better thing could he go for than a project like this?"

"I could think of lots of things."

8

KURT LIFTED HIS HAND and the yells ceased. "We need four clowns to walk on either side of the float. I've arranged for costumes at a rental agency. We have an old-fashioned bike with large front wheel fastened to the chassis ahead of old Uncle Scrooge which I'll be pedaling while waving to our public — "

Cheers and whistles drowned him out. Lynn felt the thrill of school spirit. She clapped Sherry on the back in her excitement.

38

Joel joined Kurt on the truck and lifted his hand for quiet. "I want to publicly thank Kurt for — "

"Oh, no you don't!" Kurt took a flying leap and landed halfway to the gym. "C'mon, you guys! Let's get moving!"

The boys scrambled to assemble the figures for the float.

When the truck finally took off, Jodi said, "Want a ride?"

Lynn was hesitant. "You'll never get home if you take all of us."

"Who cares?" cracked Jodi in her brittle way. "My folks are never home. They give me a car and a credit card to amuse myself. C'mon, if you're going with me.

"Carla, let me drop you off last. Maybe your mother has some of her good goulash tonight. I'm sick of those meat pies Mother keeps in the freezer. She's off somewhere with her bridge club, sipping cocktails."

Carla looked as though she had had her face lifted by some miraculous treatment.

Lynn was amazed. Carla seemed a different person. She actually smiled with a genuine expression of pleasure.

Lynn climbed in the rear of the convertible with Julie while Sherry and Carla rode in front.

Jodi plunged into thick traffic on the boulevard. Brakes screeched, horns blared, and a man slowed in front of them, making her slam her brakes.

Jodi swore and yanked the wheel to get around him. "Who does he think he is?"

The cars in the next lane honked and brakes squealed to let her in. She floored it and the car bolted ahead in a swift takeoff.

Sherry gasped, "When did you get your pilot's license?"

Jodi turned her head to smile at her and Carla yelled, "Look out!"

"I'm watching!" Jodi flung back her long hair and jolted to a stop at a red light.

Julie observed politely, "This is some car."

"Ought to be," Carla quipped. "Lamberts get the best."

Sherry said, "I don't mean to be nosy, Carla, but — well, I guess I *am!*"

"Go ahead." Carla squinted at her.

39

"Well, how come tall Jodi dates a shorty like Craig and petite Carla goes with tall Kurt?"

Lynn cringed. A glance at Julie showed her friend's consternation. Sherry might as well have inquired why the wealthy Jodi and Kurt were each dating out of their element.

Jodi snorted. "Kicks. What else?"

Carla sniffed. "Who cares?"

Sherry always had an answer. "You should really get kicks from Craig — 'the deadly tackle on our team' — and I quote from Joel's script. Boy! Am I looking forward to that game Friday night!"

"Me too."

"You can say that again!"

Jodi looked in the rear view mirror at Julie. "You can't have your club this Friday can you?"

"There's no other day open. We plan to hold a short meeting because we all have to get home and back to the field early. A doctor of science is coming. He'll only talk about ten minutes."

Sherry pointed down the street. "Here's my corner, Jodi. Just drop me here and thanks loads."

"No trouble," said Jodi. "What house?"

Sherry indicated the number. "You two sure ought to hear this guy Sunday, if you can't make it to club."

Carla yawned and looked bored. "If we're back in time. Going to N'York again."

"What's New York got that Philly hasn't?" Sherry asked as she climbed out.

Carla screeched.

Jodi flipped her black hair over her shoulders. "There're some real cool guys from the university up there. Namely Hal Chase, Kurt's brother, and — "

Carla cried, "His pal, Tony. Tony's got more up his sleeve for kicks than Craig ever dreamed of!"

Friday afternoon the student body bolted to the auditorium for a pep rally. Cheerleaders led in school yells. The band played, and Kurt Chase was called to the stage to join in a brass trio.

Lynn looked at Joel across the band section and his eyes

met hers. A slight shrug of his shoulders spoke his thoughts. Kurt was in his element. He'd never show up at club today.

When the bell rang at three-fifteen, Lynn hauled her books and clarinet case to the music room for club meeting. Pauline was already there, disapproval stamped between her brows.

Pauline faced Lynn accusingly. "I wouldn't give that Kurt Chase one slight encouraging glance if it were *me!*"

Lynn blushed, opened her mouth, then sat down and closed her eyes. *Keep still. It won't do any good to say anything.*

Her friends drifted in, chatting about the parade. Sherry said, "We'll win the prize for sure. No one but Kurt Chase could dream up such a fantastic float!"

Pauline stood by a desk, hands on hips, glaring through her stringy hair. "You and Lynn Hale are encouraging a night club entertainer. Did you know that? Your idol, Kurt, was written up in the *News* this summer as New York's youngest and *hottest* trombonist in a Manhattan night spot. And you are both condoning him and that tough character he runs with — Craig Barr!" She stopped short at the look on their faces.

Craig and Kurt stood in the door, Kurt's crooked smile indicating he had overheard. Craig snapped, "So you want me to sit in on a crummy old Bible club! Ha! I'm cutting out!" He wheeled and nearly bumped into Jodi and Carla.

Jodi talked briefly with him in the hall. Then she joined Kurt and Carla in the back row.

Joel stood at the front. "We'll not take time for any music because everyone is in a rush today. I'll turn the club over to Dr. Winkelman, our guest speaker."

The doctor had their attention for the full ten minutes. Then he prayed and the meeting was over.

Jodi left immediately, but Kurt stopped to talk with the speaker. Carla shifted from one foot to the other, listening.

Sherry glared at Pauline and her group who were flocking around the doctor. "I wish she'd get out of here! There's Kurt trying to talk to him and — "

She stopped as Joel came over. He lowered his voice, "I think Kurt and Carla will go to Kathy's Cafe with us. His

41

mother never misses a homecoming game and she wants to meet him there. See you outside in a sec."

Lynn's heart sank; her hands were clammy. Joel wasn't waiting for her as usual, and she hated to go with them to the cafe. Her father and Bernice were planning to eat there tonight.

On the front steps of the school Lynn heard Kurt and Joel shout, "Gil!" In a group at the curb, Gil's handsome head towered above the others. He looked up with a big smile and came toward them, hand in hand with an attractive girl.

Sherry muttered, "Lauren."

Joel said, "We're heading for Kathy's. Why not join us, Gil?"

Gil appealed to his friend. "They have Kosher corned beef sandwiches there, as good as Max's. Why shouldn't we? And these are wonderful people. The Evans's — you know Joel and his sister — and another friend, Lynn Hale, and Sherry, and you know Kurt already."

"Sure. I know Kurt. He's an old pal of mine." Lauren slipped an arm through Kurt's and leaned her head on his arm.

Carla tossed her tangled hair. Lauren's black hair shone in a sleek, well-kept style. Her skirt and sweater were obviously expensive. But the Jewish girl was not aloof. The girls knew she had been voted the most popular girl in school.

Lauren took Gil's hand and flashed her brilliant smile. "So, why not? Sounds good to me."

The group moved down the steps. Julie was beside Lynn when Carla's loud whisper reached them. "So, why not she says. Well, Kurt Chase, *you* can run around with Jews if you want to. Not me!"

Kurt stopped on the sidewalk, and Julie stumbled into him as the girls passed. His answer reached them clearly. "When did *you* get so good?"

Julie quickened her pace, but Sherry lagged behind. She soon caught up and did not hesitate to supply the missing details. "Did you hear — "

Julie's quick, "Yes, Sher," failed to stop her. "Is Carla

ever mad! She told him, 'and who killed Christ?' And he said in a real hard way, 'people like you — blinded by prejudice!' "

"Sherry, hush! He's right behind us," Julie cautioned.

Sherry called nonchalantly, "Hi, Kurt. Isn't Carla coming too?"

He strode past them to join Joel and Gil ahead. "I hope not!"

Lauren seemed to be doing all the talking. She kept up an animated conversation, the boys' faces turned toward her every minute.

Sherry said sourly, "I don't know why they call her the most popular girl in school. She's only friendly to the boys, that's for sure!"

Julie whispered, "Know what? I've been reading up on the Jewish religion. And Pastor gave me some good help on the subject too. Joel and I are hoping we can talk to Gil about the Lord."

Lynn saw her father ahead. "Oh, kids! There are my folks. My dad will have a busy evening. South band is joining ours at this opening game."

By the time they had found a table in the crowded cafe, Kurt's mother arrived. She acknowledged introductions cordially, removing long kid gloves carefully.

Lynn's father came in with Bernice. "The maestro himself!" Kurt cried. "Mother, this is the band leader everyone raves about — Mr. Hale. Make way, folks. We need a larger table."

"Kurt is back in orbit," Sherry mumbled. "Look! He's holding his arm for your stepmother, Lynn, acting like a waiter in some plush joint. Oh, he's the funniest thing!"

Bernice could be witty and Kurt showed appreciation for her humor. He seated Mr. and Mrs. Hale and his mother, then looked for Lynn. "Where's Red? Come down here, Lynn. Don't sit so far away."

She shook her head, but Sherry moved closer to the middle and she had to follow, which placed her opposite Kurt and Bernice.

The waitress brought ice water and menu cards. School kids filled the tables around them.

43

Mrs. Chase chatted with Bernice, and Kurt kept the girls entertained. Kurt looked at his watch. "We've got to get out of here. It's been a half hour since she took our order."

"We should have stopped at McConnel's," Bert said under his breath.

Bernice's answer carried down the table. "She'd better bring our order! We were here first!" She turned and scowled across the room at the girl who carried a loaded tray to another table.

Mrs. Chase observed quietly, "That young couple were a bit ahead of us, I believe, and they are being served now. That is fairly fast service."

Kurt caught the waitress' eye and she hurried over.

"Sorry," she told them. "We're really pushed today and one girl is sick."

Lauren said, "We understand. But tell them to make this a rush order, darling. We have members of the band who have to get on the field."

"I'll do my best," the girl murmured.

Sherry nudged Lynn on one side and Julie on the other.

Kurt, humming his theme song, and Sherry's giggle kept Lynn's dimples coming and going. She couldn't keep her face straight.

Mrs. Chase gave her son an amused look. "Did I ever teach you to whistle and hum at the table?" Her sudden smile included the girls.

"Who was hamming it up at the breakfast bar this morning, Mom?" Kurt said loudly, to be heard above the increasing din.

"You win." His mother's laugh was musical.

Two vertical lines deepening between Bernice's eyebrows forecast a storm. Lynn bit her fingernails. Bert glanced uneasily at his wife.

When the waitress brought coffee, Bernice said arrogantly, "Didn't I see you carry a tray to those boys over there? We were here long before they came in!"

"Yes, ma'am, I know. But they only ordered cokes and sandwiches. It takes longer for burgers and fries."

"Well, you'd better step on it, girl! We can't wait all day. My husband has a band to organize on the field."

44

Lynn caught the exchange of looks between Kurt and his mother. Lauren's glance at Gil revealed her disgust at Bernice's attitude. Lynn dug her fingernails into the palms of her hands.

9

JULIE BROKE THE TENSION. "We're close to the field. I'm sure we'll all get there in time."

The waitress brought Gil's order first. Lauren picked up her sandwich and cried, "Oh, no! Not cold! *Nobody* eats a *cold* corned beef sandwich. Gil, I thought you said — "

"Look! It's late. Let's forget it this time. After all — "

"Take it back. I don't want it." Lauren pushed her plate aside and the waitress slammed it to a tray.

Gil said, "How about some homemade vegetable soup? It's tops here."

The waitress said icily, "Shall I bring soup?"

"Yes, please," Gil said pleasantly, "and make that two bowls."

Joel was saying to Mrs. Chase, "I hope you meet my folks tonight. This homecoming game is the only one of the season they attend. Say! I have it! Mother is on the refreshment committee for our after-game party. Could you come over to our church with Kurt? I'll introduce you."

"We're entertaining tonight, also," Mrs. Chase said graciously. "I suggest you all come to our apartment instead. Do you young people care for pizzas?

"You see, Kurt's brother, Hal, will show up sometime in the next hour or so. He and his roommate, Tony, are coming down to see this float Kurt has been raving about. They will be in town overnight. Do come."

Lynn saw Joel hesitate. He would think of the right

45

thing to say. A glance at her stepmother's red face set her heart hammering.

Bernice took over. "These Christian young people have their *own* entertainment on game nights."

The girls watched Mrs. Chase. She remained cool, took time to finish a bite of sandwich, dabbed at her lips with a corner of her napkin, and said silkily, "My! You seem to intimate, Mrs. Hale, that we *aren't* Christians."

Bernice barged on, "I'm not talking about church membership!"

Lynn's dismay was acute as shock registered in each face. Joel's face flushed with embarrassment. Bert Hale kept eating, his eyes down. Kurt's grin turned to a sneer.

Sherry whispered, "If only she would let Joel do the talking. She's fouled it all up!"

Lynn's face betrayed her distress. Kurt noticed and his expression changed. He winked at Joel. "Joe, I like *your* brand of Christianity. What about it?"

"We'll talk about it some other time, Kurt."

Kurt returned his knowing look. Lynn breathed a sigh and relaxed.

Bernice, oblivious, kept talking. "Bert, I'm out of tracts. Do you have one to leave for the waitress? That one on God's way of salvation made plain." Then she leaned close to him and shifted her eyes upward to indicate Mrs. Chase who was standing by a chair pulling on her gloves.

Lynn wished she could run away. Everyone could see that Bernice wanted to give the tract to Mrs. Chase. Didn't she have any sense?

Suddenly Lynn understood. Spiritual discernment! Her stepmother might be able to teach music and direct choirs — she could even teach a Sunday school class — but she was not filled with the love of Christ. *Though I have . . . all knowledge . . . and have not love, I am nothing.* The familiar passage from Corinthians shot like a beam of light through her mind.

Lauren lighted a cigarette and deliberately exhaled smoke across the table. The girls heard her disgusted remark, "I'm so glad I came!"

Sherry poked Lynn. "Yow! That does it! Boy, Lynn, you

46

must have a lively time at your house. Your stepmother and Pauline are both — "

Sherry and Lynn looked up. Kurt was patting them on the shoulder. "We'll go ahead. See you out there."

Julie stood and held out her hand to Kurt's mother. "We do appreciate your kindness in asking us to come, Mrs. Chase. May we count on it some other Friday?"

Mrs. Chase's cold look thawed. "You may still come tonight, dear, if your friends would *like* to."

Joel held up a hand. "Let's take a vote. How many can make it to Chase's tonight?"

Lauren said, "Let's, Gil. I don't care about the school dance."

Gil agreed, as did the girls.

"That makes it unanimous, Mrs. Chase," Joel said with enthusiasm. "And many thanks for your hospitality."

"Don't mention it, Joel. Kurt has told me all about you interesting young people, and it is my privilege, I'm sure, to get better acquainted." Mrs. Chase gave Bernice and Bert a brief glance, icily adding, "Nice to meet you."

Bernice beamed. "We're very happy to meet you, Mrs. Chase. I hope we'll see you again soon. I'd like to have a much longer visit."

Kurt's mother darted a questioning look at her, nodded uncertainly, and followed her tall son from the room.

Bert helped Bernice with her coat. "Time we shifted into high gear," he said.

Bernice scowled. "You'd think Kurt's mother would have the courtesy to wait for me. We could have gone to the game together!"

At the football field Lynn joined her band in the opening march. From the noise of the stands she knew the floats were moving.

The band reached the goal posts and turned the corner at attention. A roar from Howard's side announced their float as Kurt pedaled from his high perch and clowns ran alongside. She scanned the bleachers near the gate for her friends who were saving her place.

Lynn saw the girls arm in arm with others in their row, swaying to the rhythm of *Howard High Forever*. Streams of colored crepe paper catapulted from the top row. Cheerleaders churned the crowd to an organized yell.

The bands dispersed and as Lynn climbed the bleachers, she saw Kurt stepping down to meet her. She accepted his outstretched hand as he pulled her beside him and pointed to a blond fellow down the row. "My brother, Hal, and his friend, Tony. Here comes Joel Evans. Have a seat, Joe — here in front of us. I reserved it for you."

A blast from the whistle indicated the game was on.

"Watch Craig!" Kurt shouted.

Lynn spotted him. Craig looked tougher than ever with shoulders and knees padded. But her attention throughout the game was focused on Kurt's brother.

Hal's hair hung long and thick on his neck line. He was growing a beard and the blond hair shone white in the floodlights. His face was grooved with long, cynical lines, and his crooked smile made her shiver. *He is wondering why Kurt is interested in us.*

Tony gestured frequently with his hands — long, slender, white hands. Tony would be handsome with that black, curly hair if he had a different expression in his roving eyes. Lynn was disgusted by his sidelong glance of cynical curiosity.

During the last half of the game, she developed an aversion to Hal's egotistical gestures and remarks. *Kurt looks clean compared with those two.*

"But he's likely to turn out just like his brother," Joel commented afterward on their way to the car. "Those universities are turning out thousands of skeptics like Hal."

"Glad we shook those guys for a few minutes. They give me the creeps," Sherry shuddered.

Julie sighed, "Let's not stay long, Joel."

He said, "I'm for giving it half an hour or so. If the conversation runs out of bounds we'll head for our party. We had to go or Mrs. Chase —"

Julie said quickly, "Now, Lynn, we all know how it is."

Lynn's throat ached. Her words were almost a whisper, "If you didn't understand, I'd die!"

They skimmed through Fairmount Park to a wide avenue.

"Wow!" Sherry cried, "Penthouse apartments. I still prefer my cozy row house on our narrow street down in civilization."

Julie sighed again. "Wonder what we'll run into tonight!"

Joel swung into the parkway surrounding the apartments.

"I don't believe Kurt will put us on the spot. He has 'good background' as Mother would say."

"Well" Sherry barked, "his brother had the same background, and look at *him!*"

A small turquoise sports car rolled alongside and honked. Joel waved and tapped his horn in response. "Gil! We'll follow him. He's been here before."

Gil drove into a corner parking lot. "We're only stopping a few minutes, Joel," he announced. "Lauren has decided to go back to the dance after all."

Lauren's smile was brilliant. "I know the homecoming queen. Congratulations, Joel! Your float took first prize. Didn't Kurt give us seniors a real send off in that deal? We'll have some good pictures for the *Annual* in June."

"I'll say." Joel was radiant. "And I saw the reporter today for Sunday's paper."

"Hi, group!" someone yelled.

"Kurt!" Gil waved.

The girls saw Hal at the wheel, with Jodi beside him. Carla was in back with Tony and Kurt. Sherry mumbled, "So Carla is *in* once more."

Lynn's heart leaped when Joel stopped and held out his hand to her. *He doesn't want Kurt to get the idea that I am unattached.* Joel knew she would want to return with her friends. He felt responsible for her safety on this venture. But no matter what the reason, she thrilled again at his firm handclasp.

Kurt led the way into the foyer. They shot to the eighteenth floor in one of the roomy elevators and padded silently down a carpeted corridor to the lavishly furnished apartment.

Mrs. Chase descended red carpeted steps from a higher level.

"Welcome everyone. Lauren, would you show the girls to my room, dear?"

The girls followed her through a short hall. The girls stood speechless in the elegant suite.

Jodi and Carla threw their wraps on the bed carelessly. Jodi seated herself at a long vanity in the adjoining room, picked up a hair brush, and pouted at her reflection. "It burns me up! That nutty Craig getting his fingers sprained. He won't get up here in time, that's for sure!"

Carla teased a strand of stiff hair. "Well, I won't ride back with Gil and Lauren! I'll take a taxi first!"

"Leave it to me, baby," Jodi laughed. "I think I'm falling in love with someone *new!*"

Carla sniffed. "Thought so. Saw it coming in N'York. Hal and you look swell together, Jodi. He's a head taller. Craig and you look more like mother and son."

"Carl!" Jodi yelped, but Carla slipped out of the room.

Lynn saw Julie nod toward the hall and followed her.

Mrs. Chase was watching for them. "I want you to see the view from our balcony before we have our buffet."

Lynn avoided Hal and Tony. Hal's conversation was constant swearing and Tony's appraisal of each girl made her cringe.

"A magnificent view!" Joel stood beside her at the wrought iron railing.

Beyond apartment buildings and trees outlining the park, they could see streaks of light made by cars on the freeway several miles distant. Turning the corner of the building gave them view of the downtown skyline.

Jodi wandered out, but Hal swept her back into the apartment. The others drifted inside, Tony close to Carla.

Lauren surveyed the loaded table. "Mrs. Chase! You said pizzas — not smorgasbord — but it's scrumptious! How about that, Gil? She even has Kosher salami. How sweet!"

"Everyone to his taste, Lauren." Mrs. Chase took a step toward Joel and Lynn. "The soft drinks are at this end of the table."

Hal's head shot up and Lynn felt his glance. His thin lips turned down in contempt for a brief instant. Then he filled his plate and sat with Jodi on a gold brocade sofa.

10

KURT SPRAWLED ON the long davenport opposite and Hal said, "Brother, you should have been with me last Sunday night. The *Basin* was doing business for real. After you guys left town, Tony and I went slumming with those girls you met on campus.

"They have this new drummer out there at the *Spot*. Burl Rosen. Can he hypnotize an audience! We sat there till four in the morning in a trance. He can do those brushes and cymbals like nobody you ever saw! The way he rattles sends me. It's the grimpiest!"

"Grimpiest?" Carla repeated.

Tony waved his sandwich and grimaced. "Hal's good at creative vocabulary. English prof likes it. Says any word, even slang, can become a part of the English language if it is *used* often enough."

"Yep," Hal said, "usage makes it correct. 'It ain't gonna rain no more' is absolutely fine now. That is, if you run with the crowd that says 'it ain't gonna.' But seriously, Kurt, the prof tells us that in about ten years he won't have to teach English anymore because of the new trend.

"Some lawyers say that our new dictionaries will corrupt the whole English language. If a word doesn't mean what it meant in past decades, law enforcement may become a farce. You couldn't convict a man without words which *mean* something — that is —"

"We get the message," Tony said. "Usage makes correct. The old values are meaningless." He moved closer to Carla. "But I'm not gonna get all shook up over it."

Mrs. Chase stood by the table, coffeepot poised over a cup. "Hal, this sounds intriguing! I had no idea such things were developing in the field of education."

51

Jodi said, "I've applied to your university, Hal. Keep your fingers crossed. I've heard it's a long waiting list."

"You'll get in, baby. I'll see the girls in the office." Hal's reply brought giggles from Carla. "What's your line?" Hal asked Joel. "News or preaching? Kurt mentioned something — 'about your newspaper work.'"

"I'm not sure whether it will be journalism or the ministry," Joel announced pleasantly.

"Do you really believe all this religious jazz. I mean the Bible being God's Word and all that jargon?" Hal asked cynically.

"Yes, I do, Hal," replied Joel seriously.

"Now wait a minute," interrupted Kurt. "You say you believe it's God's Word. How can you prove it's even true?"

Joel smiled. "You can prove it in many ways: predictive prophecies fulfilled, an accurate history of the Jewish people written two thousand years in advance, a description of the twentieth century also written thousands of years in advance, and the records of chemistry, as you heard from Dr. Winkelman, Kurt. Then there are the records of astronomy, archaeology, the science of physics, geology, and even meteorology. And, last but not least, the Bible is proved a supernatural book by personal experience."

Lynn noticed Hal's wide mouth clamped in disapproving lines. He squinted one eye at Joel. "You've got a good head, but you haven't been around, boy. My science prof could settle all your arguments."

"Try to, you mean," Joel smiled. "Haven't you heard any doctors of science who *do* believe the Scriptures?"

"He's right, Hal," Kurt offered. "This Dr. Winkelman we heard at Joe's club knew what he was talking about. Said that God measured and weighed every substance which He created. Had to, or we wouldn't be sitting here! And this prophet, Isaiah, couldn't possibly have known the chemical secrets mentioned in his book because science hadn't caught up with the Bible account in that day and time. Man! I wish you could have heard him. I can't begin to tell about it."

Hal's chin shot up. "This English prof — the one I mentioned — he's tops! Got us to read and read and read some more. Shoved us into a wider outlook. Sure, the Bible is great literature and its concept is necessary for *some* people, even in this enlightened age of scientific discovery.

"But those of us who have the courage to think for ourselves are able to overcome this guilt complex — it can drive a person to insanity! He told us to throw away our crutches, whatever they were. 'If it's your parents' old-fashioned ideas about God — throw them away. Become a new person. Your mind can begin to soar to heights you never dreamed possible.' I tell you, man, I'm real gone on this.

"This same prof," he caught Jodi's eye, "is the one who's all for our little project. He's willing to try anything new. He's really open-minded to discover — well, Truth, if you will. Anyway, I've been set free from such prudish nonsense."

Joel looked at him thoughtfully. "Only the power of God can set us free."

Lauren scrambled to her feet. "You should talk to my rabbi. I let him do all my thinking about the Almighty. Come on, Gil, we'd better get to the dance."

Mrs. Chase followed the girls as they too gathered their things to leave. "This has been a most interesting discussion. I had intended to leave you young people alone for the evening, but the conversation held me spellbound! I want you to come back and try it again sometime. Kurt has talked of nothing but your club and certain of its members." She smiled at Lynn.

Lynn shook hands and murmured her thanks.

Kurt dashed into the elevator with them. "Mind if I go along? Tony says they'll come by and pick me up in an hour. Okay?"

"Sure thing." Joel looked at his watch. "That will be about right."

The minute they reached the church, Sherry led the girls to the powder room. "My hair looks a sight. That old wind whipped it like an egg beater. Boy! I can't stand that Hal! He has a way of putting you down like you're some kind of worm."

Julie admitted, "He is rather obnoxious."

Lynn sighed. "But wasn't it interesting? And Kurt remembered what he heard at our club!"

Julie said, "I believe Gil would have stayed if Lauren hadn't gotten restless."

Sherry winked at Lynn. "It's always the girls who grimp everything up."

"Sherry, you're a riot!"

"Let's join the gang."

The ping-pong tables were all in use. They looked around for the boys and got in line with them to shoot darts.

Lynn noticed Pauline Porter's dark glance. When the girls changed to table games, Pauline sauntered over to ask, "Why were you so late?"

Sherry's freckled nose wrinked comically. "Were we late?"

Pauline twitched her shoulders in disgust and marched off.

In the middle of their game refreshments were announced. Kurt looked up, annoyed. "I'm not hungry."

Joel said, "We can at least take a coke —" then stopped short. Angry voices sounded from the stairway. They heard someone holler, "*Kurt!*"

"Sounds like Craig!" Kurt reached the hall in long strides.

Lynn and Sherry hurried to the double doors on their side of the room. An odor of alcohol seeped in with Craig and his three friends. Craig waved his arm and shouted at Kurt, "All right, pal! Where ish Jodi? What the —"

Kurt's long arm shot out and pushed him back. "Shut up! This is a church!"

Craig swore. "Shut up! Thish ish a church!" He slapped one of the fellows on the shoulder and laughed.

Julie slipped behind Lynn. Sherry gasped, "He's drunk! And his right hand is bandaged."

"Oh, no!" Julie's backward glance turned their attention. Pauline, followed by her friends, swept past them to see what was going on.

Lynn flattened her back against the wall and held her breath as Pauline marched up to Craig's gang and stood there, hands on hips.

"Where ish she?" Craig blocked Kurt like a tackle on field. "Why didn't she tell me where she wash goin' huh? What ya tryin' ta pull, ye big s'phisticated lout!"

A fellow with a thick mat of hair hanging in his eyes

54

approached Pauline. She screamed and then caught sight of Joel in the doorway. "Get your bums out of here!"

Craig's thick arms encircled her shoulders, and her scream turned to a gasp as his hold became painful. The girls watched helplessly as she moved her head back and forth in frantic jerks.

Kurt's demand, "Let her go!" only brought the circle of hoodlums tighter around Craig.

One of the youth sponsors cried out, "What's going on out here?"

Craig dropped his arms and Pauline slapped him across the mouth.

"I'll tell —" her words ended in a shriek. Craig gave her wrist a wrench and flung her against the wall. Pauline's eyes blazed as she leaned there shaken and panting.

Craig called over his shoulder, "You asked for it, sis. And I'm not through wish you, preacher Paul -*een*. Got a li'l surprise saved up for ya." His laugh was crude and mirthless.

Kurt's face was red with anger. "Get out of here, Craig Barr! You're potted!"

"Oh, no, I ain't. Haven't even smoked it today. You can —"

Kurt's fist cracked Craig's chin; Craig sagged into the arms of a pal behind him.

The sponsor cried out, "All *right,* boys! Break it up! Clear out!"

Craig lunged at Kurt. His bandaged hand shot out and connected. Craig howled in pain, his oaths horrible to hear.

The sponsor uttered the word "police" and two fellows lunged toward the stairs. Craig slunk after his friends, Kurt and Joel on their heels.

Joel stood on the steps outside and called after them: "What do you mean, Craig Barr, entering a church and disturbing our youth group?"

Craig muttered, "I only wanted to see Kurt on a li'l business — thash all."

Kurt was furious. "I'm not your baby-sitter, Craig! If Jodi likes Hal, what do you expect me to do?"

"She didn't show at the dance. Your ma said they left your place an hour ago. I want ta know what thish —"

"Aw, kill it! Let's blow!" The bearded fellow punched Craig's arm. "She ain't here!"

The fellows moved down the street. In the shadows down the block car doors slammed. The roar of an unmuffled motor and the screech of tires broadcast their departure.

The sponsors came out. "Did they leave? Good. Now, Joel, Pauline is injured. Her wrist seems to be sprained."

Sherry cried, "It's all her fault! She never knows when to leave people alone."

The sponsor gave her a cool look without comment and returned to the basement.

Kurt's eyes narrowed. "Joe, I'm sorry. That's all I can say."

"It wasn't your fault. We know that."

"I'll phone your pastor and explain so you won't get the blame, Joe. Craig drinks too much — looks like Jodi is shaking him for my brother."

"Isn't that Hal now pulling up at the curb?"

Kurt seemed to react slowly. "Yeah. Well, see you around, Joe. I'll stay away from here — never be able to live it down."

"Kurt, no!" Joel leaped after him.

Kurt opened the rear door and climbed in.

Lynn whispered, "Everyone will blame Joel for this. We've got to stand together."

The car pulled away. Joel walked slowly back to them, shoulders sagging.

11

KURT WAS DIFFERENT the following week. Lynn felt it mainly because he did not stop to talk with her as usual. He needed a hair cut and a shave. When their eyes met, he gave her a crooked smile and a short jerk of the hand which resembled a salute.

Joel's grave smile told her he also noticed.

When classes were dismissed in midmorning for assembly, the three met in the hall.

Kurt seemed his natural self. "Sit with us, Lynn lovely?"

Joel frowned, but Kurt insisted that she sit between them. "Carla and I broke up," he explained. "She's mad about Tony. What she doesn't know — he has a campus steady. He's just out for kicks. Anyhow, I was fed up with Carla's capers. How about a date for —"

Joel leaned forward. "I think you should know, Kurt, that Lynn and I have gone together for two years, ever since she moved north."

Kurt grinned at Lynn. "Oh, ah knew she was from the saouth," he drawled.

Lynn couldn't stop smiling. Joel's remark set everything right again. He said, "Kurt, do you always have to go up to New York on Friday night? We'd like you to go to church with us some Sunday."

"Look, kids! Let me fill you in. Now I don't want to hurt or disillusion anyone, but I saw two fellows in your youth group Friday night — two guys and one little gal — all from my section of town. One guy's father is a deacon in your church. And I see him at the night spots both here *and* N'York."

Kurt stopped when the assembly was called to order. Afterward, on their way down the hall, he continued, "And that shortie with the pixie hairdo — *brother!* That girl is no Christian. You should see her cut up at parties where — well, never mind. You kids haven't grown up yet. Lynn, you'll have to excuse me, but you just don't have the big picture."

Lynn met his eye steadily. "Kurt, we already knew. What *you* have to learn is: not every church member is a Christian who allows God to run his life. And every church has at least one member who may not be a believer at all!"

Before they separated for classes Joel said, "When you find three or four rotten potatoes in a bag, do you throw them all away?"

In Bible club the last week of October Joel announced, "Last chance for youth retreat reservations. We're going to have a big time at our camp on the lake. Of course, it'll include a Halloween party, and we'll have a hay ride to start with. Since Thursday and Friday are teachers' convention, we'll meet early Thursday morning. Pick up your registration cards here after the meeting. There's a list of what to wear and what to bring. Above all, bring a friend. Yes, Pauline?"

"I think we'd better be careful who we invite. We don't want to spoil it for *good* contacts we have made. I have two girls from my neighborhood who are coming with me, but if their mothers thought we would be subjected to a scene such as we had in church one Friday night in September —"

Joel interrupted, "I don't believe you have anything to be worried about, Pauline."

Lynn happened to look back and caught a glimpse of Carla's face at the door window. Carla looked unhappy. A certain wistfulness in the girl's glance struck a responsive chord. Lynn had to know.

Carla was halfway down the hall when Lynn reached her. "Carla, wait!" *What should she say? Why had she followed Carla? Bring a friend.* Joel's voice played back in her mind. She said, "Please join us. We're planning a good time this weekend — a camp-out at Cedar Lodge on Cedar Lake. Wouldn't you like to go?"

Carla didn't respond with her usual brassy comeback. She cocked her head to one side and looked dubious. "Who cares? What does it matter to *you* whether I come or not?"

"It matters, Carla. It's hard to explain, but we all care — those of us who know the Lord in a personal way — and we want others to know Him as we do. It means everything, Carla, to know the love of God. *He* cares about you."

Carla looked down at her feet. Then she looked up again with the wistful air that had struck Lynn so strangely. "Well, kid, I'll admit I'd like to try something new for a change. Something's been bugging me." She walked beside Lynn to the music room.

Lynn led her to a seat in the back. She wished Pauline and her two friends would keep their faces to the front. Their stares and disapproving glances could only hinder the Lord's work.

Joel drove Lynn home after school. He was enthusiastic. "Talk about answered prayer! And if you hadn't noticed her at that moment — Lynn, will you pray with me about Kurt? I'm going to try once again to interest him in going with us. Say! If *you'd* ask him —"

"No, Joel. It isn't fair. He'll think I care about him, and I don't want to lead him on. You know it isn't right."

"You're right. It isn't right."

He stopped the car in front of her house. She waited. Joel always held her hand and gave her an extra special look when they parted. This time he stared ahead, not touching her. The premonition returned; something was on his mind — something which separated them. Sudden tears smarted her eyes.

Lynn grabbed her books, flung open the door before he could come around to her side, and called back. "Thanks and bye" as she ran up the steps.

She slipped up the front stairs but stopped as Bette ran out of their room. The girl pushed her rudely. Lynn's notebook fell, scattering loose papers in the hall.

"Oh, I hate you, Lynn Hale! You didn't iron my best blouse like Mom told you to, and now I'll be late for Joan's party!"

Lynn stooped to gather the papers. Her stepsister's words added to the frustration from Joel's strange behavior choked her.

Bette demanded in the same tone her mother used, "Aren't you going to say something? Answer me!"

Bernice's shrill voice rasped, "Never mind. I'll iron it for you. We can't expect Miss Goldilocks to bother herself with it!" She appeared in the doorway. "Lynn, you speak to your sister this minute! None of your high-hat actions when I'm here!"

Lynn's voice was strained and thin. "I'm sorry. I didn't mean to forget it this morning."

"No, I dare say you didn't *mean* to." Bernice and Bette both laughed in derision. "You just conveniently forgot, that's all."

Lynn stared at them in horror. How could they judge her motives so harshly! Anger leaped through her grief. She

59

cried, "Both of you despise me. You don't believe anything I say!"

She heard her father's step in the hall. Fear clutched her. As usual, he only heard her outburst. And Bernice took advantage of the situation. She fled downstairs calling back to Lynn, "Is that a Christian attitude to have after all I've done to make a home for you?" Then a faked sob, "Bert, I don't know what more I can do. I've done my best to help and train that girl, and she simply will not cooperate. She can't say a kind word to me — just goes to her room the minute she gets through with any little task I assign her. I don't know what I've done to cause her to be upset. She flies off the handle so easily —" a pause and another sob, "I just don't know what more I can do."

Lynn, trembling at the door of her room, heard his usual command, "Lynn, come down here!"

Bette disappeared into the bathroom.

Lynn walked unsteadily to the stairs, mechanically descended, and faced them.

"She looks ill," he remarked to Bernice.

Bernice raised her voice. "You are taking *her* part — against *me?*" The woman's body was rigid, her head swayed, and her narrowed eyes held Bert's until he turned on Lynn.

"Why do you upset Bernice? You know better. Go to your room and stay there!"

Lynn mounted the stairs; her feet seemed too heavy to move. Bernice's harsh laugh rang in her ears, "What an easy out! I never had it that good in my day. Bert, you make me laugh!"

He raised his voice and Lynn caught her breath when he flared back. The neighbors couldn't help but hear these arguments which increased in intensity. *I can't remember one time he ever spoke a harsh word to my own mother.*

The friction in this harassed household was sending her father into quick rages. Often he apologized, but had Bernice ever apologized for her behavior? Lynn stared at the falling leaves outside her window. She tried to remember. Had her stepmother ever admitted losing her own sense of balance? She sometimes admitted being nervous, but always blamed it on something or someone else. "I blew my top, Bert, but you should have seen the way your daughter acted."

Bert had never seen. It seemed he was always away from the house when she and Bernice had an upset. The minute he walked in the door, Bernice's attitude changed. But lately she had been turning on him too, her sharp tongue causing him to rail back.

Lynn sank down on the bed and lay quietly to ease an increasing throb in her head. She heard Bernice's sharp voice. Bette banged down the steps. Finally the sounds subsided and she dozed.

"Lynn?" Her room, shrouded in evening dusk, made her father a gray silhouette in the door.

She whispered, "Yes, Dad?"

He left the door open a crack and sat down on the edge of Bette's bed. "I didn't lose my temper like that down in Virginia. What is happening to us?"

"I don't know, Dad. I was just thinking the same thing. Where — is she —"

"In the basement. I'm worried about you, Lynn. You look exhausted these days. I think you need — wait!" They heard Bernice's step on the stairs. "We'll talk later, honey." He reached over and squeezed her arm.

"I love you," she whispered.

He closed the door silently and Lynn smiled in the shadows. *He feels it too — something is radically wrong with our home life. We are at every church service — everyone busy and smiling — but that isn't Christianity.*

She jumped up and turned on her desk light. She had better get some studying done. Two exams were coming up. After that she could look forward to the retreat — away from this house that wasn't *home.*

12

EARLY THURSDAY MORNING Lynn's father drove her to the church. She stacked her sleeping bag and overnight case with the others piled outside the bus.

Sherry was talking with Ron and Roger. Julie ran over to her, "Guess what, Lynn! I'm holding my breath until Carla gets here. She said she'd ride with us, but guess who's driving her over! Kurt! And we thought they'd broken up."

Lynn saw Joel with the boys. "Did Joel —"

"Yes, he's been talking a lot with Kurt. But Kurt, of course, considers this retreat of ours kid stuff. Said something about playing in a band in the Bronx every weekend for the rest of the school year. So that checks him out of our club, our Saturday rallies, Sunday nights and — here they are now."

Lynn put on a smile she didn't feel to greet Carla. Kurt called from the car, "C'mere, Lynn! Wanta tell you something."

Lynn kept smiling and stayed where she was. He left the car double-parked, bolted over, took her arm, and led her away from the girls. "Look, Lynn, I'm really getting involved with your group. Joel has something that gets through to me. And I want to spend more time with you — all of you — but what I'm really trying to say — Carla wanted to tell me something so I brought her over this morning. Now, Lynn, remember this! Listening?"

She nodded. He said intensely, "Carla has things all wrong about Hal and his crowd at the university. Some people can take their advanced philosophies and some can't. That's the long and short of it. Carla is basically from the — well the proletariat, as Hal says. But, Lynn, I'm trying to tell you not to pay attention to anything she tells about her trips to New York. Right?"

62

He stammered something else as Joel trotted over to say hello. Kurt gave her a crooked smile as he turned away.

Lynn noticed the bright sunshine after that. It lifted her morale to see Kurt's self-assurance deflated. At the same time she was on the alert for Carla. *I must make her feel welcome.*

Sherry left her with Carla until they arrived at camp, but they were soon thrown together when one of the leaders read the list of names for cabins. Sherry flung her navy boy's cap in the air and shouted, "Glory be! We have Miss Lindy in our cabin. Oh, Lindy, I love you!" She threw her arms around the little lady and Miss Mapes laughed.

Lynn introduced Carla and everyone carried luggage into the cabins. The chill in the autumn air kept them moving briskly.

It was a golden weekend. October's skies remained a vivid blue. The four girls sensed Carla's spiritual hunger and were not surprised when she broke down Saturday night.

Miss Lindy was reading from the Psalms before lights out, her back stiff and straight as she sat on her lower bunk bed. " 'Blessed is the man that walketh not in the counsel of the ungodly . . . nor sitteth in the seat of the scornful. But his delight is in the law of the Lord . . . and he shall be like a tree planted by the rivers of water.' Why, my dear girl, what is it?"

Miss Lindy laid down her Bible and held out her hands. Carla, sobbing as though her heart was breaking, dropped to the floor and put her head on the bed. Miss Lindy turned off the lamp and the full moon cast a silver shaft through their cabin window.

The girls climbed into their bunks, but everyone was wide-awake. Miss Lindy wrapped a blanket around Carla.

The shuddering stopped and Carla's upturned face glistened wet in the moonlight. She stammered, "That's just what they're doing. Oh, God! I'm worried about Jodi!"

"Doing what, dear?" Miss Lindy stroked her head.

Carla looked up at the shadowy bunks. "If I didn't know you girls, I wouldn't say anything. But I think — I mean, I'm pretty sure you'll understand. You — you're real Christians."

63

Julie said softly, "We all love you, Carla, and we've been praying for you. You and Jodi."

Carla began to cry again. "They believe those professors. Men who don't believe in God. They scorn the Bible — just like you read to us tonight. What I mean — Lynn, Julie, you know Jodi's running around with Hal.

"But first, Miss Lindy," and the four girls leaned from their bunks to hear, "when Dr. Winkelman was speaking tonight I bowed my head and told God I needed Christ as my Saviour. I've never felt this warmth in my heart before."

The girls gasped their delight and piled out of their bunks, all talking at once. Lynn threw her arms around Carla. "We all knew the same joy of the Lord when Jesus came into *our* lives."

Miss Lindy was radiant. Her white hair shone silver in the moonlight. "His Spirit bears witness with our spirit that we are the children of God, as the Bible says. And God promises that nothing and no one will separate a child of His from the love of God in Christ Jesus our Lord. Carla, you are His. His Spirit has entered your life.

"Now what is troubling you about your friends, dear?"

Carla tucked her feet under her quilted robe and leaned her arms across her knees. "It's sorta hard to describe. Hal calls it SR — for *Spiritual Renaissance*. But it really is known as *League for Spiritual Discovery* — from the name of the drug LSD.

"Jodi practically worships Hal. She sat at his feet while he recited Hindu prayers and it all sounded so mystical that I was really excited about it — at first."

"Go on!" Sherry bounced and the springs of the old bed creaked.

Carla sighed. "It sounded perfectly logical. Hal is a cool operator. He talked about chains of religion which keep us slaves to society. He said our conscience is fear forced on us by prudish parents or churches.

"He said we couldn't delve into the 'mysteries of expanded consciousness' until we shook our childish inhibitions. First we had to join the crowds of 'enlightened youth' who were really in the *know*. He took us to a mod shop for costumes

64

because he said 'you can't go without being dressed to relate to the mood.'

"It was fun. Jodi dressed up in a knit pajama suit of black and yellow tiger stripes. With her long black hair it looked sharp. I chose a sheath of gold metallic cloth, a gigantic gold belt, and green boots. The idea was to climb outside of ourselves — be someone entirely different.

"When Tony and Hal and Craig — and Kurt — met us at the door, they were strangers too. They looked so different. When we got there, Hal urged us to 'let ourselves go' and not think of the time or each other.

"We put on dark glasses and entered this club. The next thing I knew we were swallowed in the mob — hundreds of kids packed inside. We got separated and I was scared to death at first. There're all these colored strobe lights flashing on and off, and at first it nearly drives you crazy. It takes time to recognize the jazz because the sights and sounds are abstract — nothing related. Rhythm dominates your mind — that and the smoke we had before we went in. Weird pictures — grotesque figures moving — the weed really turns you on. I couldn't control myself. It was like being under another power.

"Miss Lindy, now I feel a strange quiet power in me. I really believe that some horrible spirit took control of me in the places we went. It was frightening.

"We were in this nightclub till almost daylight, and after I came out I was exhausted. I slept on the floor in someone's apartment — didn't care where I was or anything.

"But Hal said we were just beginning. Next weekend we were going to rid ourselves of what he called 'neurological fixes' about conscience. He said 'shake off the past. You're in a new world — no time for puritanical prudery!' "

Miss Lindy arched her back and sniffed. "And they call this a *spiritual* discovery?"

"It turned out to be my spiritual discovery, but not the way Hal thought." The girls moved closer around Carla. "Hal said we were ready for more experiments with 'total recreation,' and we were all for it. I was real high — being in with college kids. Real cool guys, I thought.

"Then Hal said, 'Don't be afraid to try *anything*.' Understand?"

The girls nodded. "Keep going," Julie urged.

"He said our grandparents were horrified when they saw a girl with a cigarette. And illegal beer parties? Shame! 'But we've made real progress. Take marijuana, for instance. People are prejudiced against that just like they used to be with alcohol and sex.'

"So I discovered that the *in* group at the university, the intellectuals like Hal, were proud of shaking their inhibitions or restrictions of any kind. Why, ordinary smoking and drinking kids were small-time. Now the pot smokers are even more popular than students from the frats and sororities.

"Hal is against social frats. Boasted that in his frat status is based only on scholastic abilities. Miss Lindy, its guys like Hal, the ones who get top grades mostly, who are going in for marijuana and LSD.

"But Jodi still isn't satisfied. She goes overboard on anything. I heard Hal on the phone and he said, 'It isn't my fault, buddy. If Jodi wants to hit the needles, that's her hard luck. I'm too smart to get hooked on the hard stuff.'"

Miss Lindy murmured, "But he headed her in that direction. It *is* his fault."

Julie whispered, "Carla — have you —"

"Yeah. Like I said, I got turned on smoking the stuff. But afterward — all week at school I was terribly depressed because life was too blah. I was a beast at home. My parents didn't know what to do with me. Finally Mom told me I couldn't go away on another weekend and I swore and said I'd knock her down if she got in my way. Boy! Won't she see a difference *now?*"

Miss Lindy covered Carla's hand with her own. "My dear, the Bible tells us that Satan transforms himself as an angel of light. These young people are being led astray, thinking they will find a new spiritual level never before achieved by man. This is why they call it a 'spiritual discovery.' How tragic!"

Carla continued, "I know I met God here. For the first time I'm not afraid of either life or death. Maybe I can show you the difference. I went on a 'trip.' It was my first and my last. What a hideous nightmare! That LSD changed my mind about Hal's marvelous mystic order. He kept telling us he knew better than to take an overdose. Maybe they could regulate it better when they used to drop the liquid on sugar cubes — I don't know — but Hal had it in capsules. We all sat in a circle around lighted candles, chanting Hindu poetry, and rocking like a bunch of weirdies.

"Hal put on a symphony record and gathered large paintings around on the floor — propped up against the couches — because he said we would see and hear everything with vision and insight beyond the realm of ordinary perception.

"I was so excited I popped it in my mouth and sat there waiting for the miracle to happen. Afterward he said I probably got too much of the stuff, but I told him he could take his junk and feed it to some other sucker. Never again!"

Sherry stirred impatiently. "What *happened?*"

13

THE GIRLS HUDDLED in a tighter ring around Carla.

"It's weird sitting here!" Sherry shivered. "Like telling ghost stories."

Carla pulled the blanket closer. "I've tried to forget what I saw in that dream. The psychiatrist Mom took me to said — but anyway, I'd like you to know the rest.

"You see, it wasn't that way at first. It took about forty-five minutes for the stuff to work. We sat in a circle on the floor, and something takes over your body. You begin to feel buzzy inside and your mind becomes lighter than air. You feel like you could run for miles on a cloud, or jump as high as the moon, or else sleep for a month. Nothing seems impossible.

"Hal was supposed to watch us, but Jodi walked right out the door and was headed straight for the four lane highway when they caught her and brought her back. She could easily have been killed.

"Did you girls know she was high when you got in her car that day after school?" Carla asked.

"No!"

"Not *really!*"

"I mean it. She doesn't see the harm in it. I was scared of the stuff. But Jodi bought some stuff in Times Square and she smokes 'em during the week. Now she's spending a lot of time with some millionaire's son. She says they're living it up, but from what I know they're trying to see how fast they can kill themselves. She isn't nice to me anymore either. They were all disgusted at my reaction to my 'trip'."

"What happened?" Sherry wailed.

Miss Lindy frowned. "Perhaps you had better not tell about it since your doctor advised you to forget."

Carla considered a moment. A light seemed to glow from her eyes. "But honestly, Miss Lindy, I feel entirely different about it since I asked God to save me from my sins. You know what? I *am* new! I'm not terrified to think about that awful night. Oh, Miss Lindy, is this deep peace His Spirit — in me?"

"Yes, Carla, dear. The Holy Spirit definitely brings quietness and assurance into our inner consciousness."

Lynn's heart leaped with a new hope. She would ask Miss Lindy about *her* problem before this weekend was over.

Carla squealed. "Oh, I'm so happy! We paid that psychiatrist thirty smackers to tell me to forget the past, but he couldn't give me the peace I needed! Oh, Lynn! What if you hadn't come out in the hall to talk with me? What if I had missed this retreat!"

They all talked at once. Then Julie said, "We'd better let Miss Lindy get some sleep."

Sherry cried, "Just tell us as fast as you can, Carla! What did it do to you?"

Carla uncurled herself and stood, silhouetted in the light from the window. Her voice sounded flat as though she had grown numb. "A piece of my childhood came out of nowhere. It was more real than when it happened years ago.

68

The people were giants, and I was like a mouse in a corner surrounded by an army of cats and dogs.

"But the people were the same as I remembered them. Girls and boys who made fun of me for being a *Polack*. Their faces were distorted. Their voices were amplified a hundred times. I covered my head with my arms to stop them from yelling at me, but they kept screaming, 'You dirty Polack!' And their laughter got so loud I couldn't stand it. I screamed and screamed.

"Hal says they held me and tried to make me take a sedative, but I fought them off. They said I finally sank into a corner and groaned there the whole night long! That was when I had the most terrifying feeling of all. I went through all the inward humiliation and fears that I had when I was a little kid — only this time it was like under a magnifying glass. I thought 'if I can pull my soul back, I'll kill myself.' You see, I knew that part of me was out there somewhere floating around, and I couldn't get it back. Oh, God."

The girls scrambled to their feet and surrounded her. Carla came back with a start. "Please — I'm okay. Honest, kids, it doesn't hurt me at all now, thank God. But that night was nothing but torture.

"Ya know, Miss Lindy, the doctor says it's a dangerous thing to fool around with acids that can disorient the mind.

"Of course Hal insisted that only one in a dozen people have a bad experience like mine, but the doctor said it's a far higher percentage than guys like Hal will admit. Craig and Kurt made light of the whole thing. But I began to get scared of *myself*, 'cause in the back of my mind I was sure I'd promised my inner self that I would destroy my body and I didn't know how to escape.

"Mom didn't know what to do with me, so we saw this psychiatrist. He had the diagnosis, but I found the cure at camp! God was looking for me and showed me the answer. Christ suffered to set me free from such sin and darkness of soul as this, and I'm not lost anymore. I'm *saved!*"

Lynn kept her arm around Carla. "He did make you whole. You are all back together in one piece: body, soul, and spirit."

69

Julie cried, "It's almost two o'clock in the morning. Miss Lindy, we must get you to bed."

"Yes, you girls had better go to breakfast without me tomorrow. I'm afraid I shall oversleep. Good night, Carla. We'll have many more long talks together now, won't we?"

Lynn called from her top bunk, "I'll bring you a tray later in the morning, Miss Lindy." She hoped she would have this teacher to herself for a little while; the burden of her own problems at home weighed heavily.

Sunday morning after early breakfast the girls dashed around preparing for church. Lynn looked in their cabin and found Miss Lindy dressed and reading her Bible. Her smile brought tears to Lynn's throat. She must get advice, and there was no other person in the world in whom she would rather confide than the godly woman who shared their cabin.

She sat beside the lady and breathed in the comfort of the quiet room. "Miss Lindy, your face always reminds me of words from Isaiah about 'the beauty of holiness.' I have to ask you something. I can't go back home until I know what to do about — well, it's my stepmother. I've never told anyone all about it. It isn't easy to explain.

"Pastor has been giving us messages on the deeper life. I've confessed each fault and sin to God and I know He forgives. But I'll fail again when I get home. I always get so nervous when she keeps at me — I begin to tremble for fear of what she'll tell my father. You see, she doesn't seem to believe that I'm trying to help. And I do try. I do! God knows — " Lynn buried her face in her arms and the tears flowed. Miss Lindy's tender hand on her head reassured her. "If it weren't for the Bible club and the Evans' family in the church, I know I would have left home a long time ago."

Miss Lindy looked beyond her. Her answer was low. "That happened to Hagar, didn't it, Lynn? She was running away from a mistress who was not treating her right, but the Lord said, 'Return and submit.' Then when the right time came, He told her it was better to leave Sarah's house.

"Hannah suffered under the lash of a woman's tongue.

70

But God was training Hannah for a special service, wasn't He?"

"Miss Lindy, it isn't only the pressure that worries me. Believe me, sometimes I'm afraid I'll crack up! I mean — lose my mind. When she gets angry — oh, Miss Lindy, I don't *like* to tell anyone all this. It's only because I've got to have help or I can't go on. I just can't go on!"

"Lynn, let me read a verse which helped me. You know, my dear, I think I'll confide something to you which I've kept hidden for many years. It's hard to thank God for the Laban in your life. Remember the shameful way Jacob's Uncle Laban treated him? Yet God allowed it, that He might make the scheming boy, Jacob, into Israel, a prince with God.

"Now, dear, I was an orphan, and I had a selfish old uncle who was my guardian. When I was eighteen years of age, a handsome young man wanted to marry me, but my uncle made me believe he would become ill and die if I should leave him. He was jealous of that young man's affections." She paused and looked through the window.

"That's the reason you never married?" Lynn whispered, covering Miss Lindy's hand with her own.

"Yes. But hear the rest of the story. My young man waited two full years for me. I still felt it my duty to stay where I was, for every day my uncle reminded me that he had given me a home.

"The very month that my young gentleman left town and married another girl, my uncle died."

"Oh, Miss Lindy!" Lynn sensed the bitter disappointment.

"Lynn, dear, what sweetened the bitter waters for the children of Israel? The rod. And only the cross will sweeten your life. You see, Lynn, what happened was God's will for *me*. Do you know what I discovered soon after my uncle's death? That I had a strange ailment, and all my life I would have to fight this affliction. I would never have held up under the stress of rearing children, and that would have caused me far more suffering. And it is wonderful to know Him, and the power of His resurrection, and the fellowship of His sufferings."

Again the lady paused and looked far away. "Dear, *dear*

71

Miss Lindy. God has used you to help many girls — more daughters than you could ever have had. You have more blessing in your life than many married people, that is certain. You mean as much to me right now as my own mother. And I loved her with all my heart."

Miss Lindy bowed her head to hide her emotion. Then she dabbed at her nose with a lacy handkerchief and straightened her back. "Now for that verse in Isaiah: 'And the work of righteousness shall be peace: and the effect of righteousness quietness and assurance forever.'

"Lynn, you spoke several times of 'fears.' The Lord came to give us the supernatural peace of God. More than that, He *is* our peace. Christ in you is your peace. I can tell you it works, for I've experienced His peace in the pain of bewilderment, in misunderstandings, in strife.

"You go home and let Christ respond when your stepmother speaks to you. Rest in Him. Believe that He is all you need for any situation. 'As you have received Him (by faith) so walk in Him.' Day by day, moment by moment."

As the bus rumbled home, Lynn felt like singing. Carla's experience of joy was her own. A thrill of anticipation kept her animated for the entire ride.

Sherry whistled. "Wowie-do, Lynn Hale! I've never seen you so full of fun. That retreat sure sent you, that's for sure!"

Sherry settled back. "Look at that wind outside. Begins to blow like November." She closed her eyes. "I can't get that poor little rich girl with the long black mane out of my mind."

Lynn watched the leaves swirling in the gusts. "I can't, either. Every time I think of Jodi I believe God puts her on my heart to pray."

Sherry sighed, "We were wrong about the bleached blond — thought she was so hard. Well, you never know."

14

LYNN KEPT WATCHING KURT at band Monday to see if he knew. Joel cautioned the girls to let Carla do the talking about what had happened.

When Kurt strolled in with his trombone, Joel called, "Hi, Kurt," and was answered by a gesture and a jerk of Kurt's head.

Lynn knew he was avoiding her eyes. She concentrated on tuning her clarinet until the band leader tapped his baton. She glanced over at Kurt and their eyes met for an instant. His sober-faced wink changed her complexion, and when she saw this pleased him, she lost even more composure.

If Joel sees me blush every time Kurt looks at me, he'll think I'm in love with the guy. She spent the rest of the hour looking at her music.

In the cafeteria line she ran into Carla. Sherry waved to them from a table and called, "Hurry up." Carla waved back. "Are you kidding? In this line?" But her brown eyes were smiling under their dark brows.

Lynn was relieved to see that her hair looked better.

Carla leaned close to her. "Lynn, Jodi isn't here today and Kurt avoided me all morning. In American History he didn't even look at me. But I'll tell him all about it when I get the chance."

"We're all praying for you, Carla. What did your mom and dad think?"

"They were all ears. Mom about flipped 'cause she thought I became a Christian when I joined our church years ago. But I told her I never met *Christ* before. Dad said he'd just as soon I go to Grace with you as to weekend parties in N'York. He thought it was a lot safer." Carla laughed with her sudden exuberance. Suddenly her face changed. "There's Gil with Joel. Oh, Lynn! I'm ashamed! Do you think he heard what I said about Jews that day?"

"I hope not. Carla, did you ever read the Book of Romans in the New Testament? Paul, who was a Jew and went to Hebrew school like Gil, wrote that God loves the Jews and has not cast away His people because they are spiritually blind. Our pastor is speaking on the subject next Sunday. If only Joel can interest Gil in coming, I'm sure he will see — Oh! I'd better hush. Here they come."

Joel called. "Join us right after lunch in the hall."

Lynn wondered why. They hurried and were in the hall by the drinking fountain talking with Sherry and Julie when the boys came out.

Joel's smile was for Carla. "Gil and I were talking, and he had the idea that all Gentiles were Christians. So he thinks those people who killed millions of his race were all Christians simply because they weren't Jews!"

"But you explained it; so I see it now." Gil smiled politely.

"Well, I want you to *really* see." Joel looked at Carla.

Lynn admired the girl. She wasn't afraid to speak, but she was searching for words. It was her first testimony at school.

"Gil, you've gotta believe it — knowing Jesus as a Friend — a real Person — has changed my whole outlook on life. Gil, I belonged to a church which has millions of followers. I saw pictures of Christ and the holy family every day of my life. I knew prayers from a prayer book, but I didn't know God.

"At camp this past week I met Christ for the first time and found that He is the only One who can bring me to God — not a church nor any other person."

Gil, usually sharp with answers, groped for something to say. "So you believe like Joel now?" He scratched his forehead with the end of his pencil. "So maybe all Christians aren't Jew haters. Joel is different. And you *have* changed, Carla." He gave her a searching look.

"I don't hate anyone or any nationality any more," she told him. "I have the love of Jesus in my heart. He changed me."

74

"That's what I've been trying to tell him," Joel said. "Real Christians love the Jews because Christ, the Hebrew Messiah, changes their hearts. If you'll read that New Testament I gave you, you'll see what we're talking about, Gil."

"I am reading it."

Julie sparkled. "Gil, we'd love to have you visit our club this Friday."

"And our church Sunday," added Sherry.

"Thank you, thank you! I'll see." Gil laughed good-naturedly. He lingered until the bell sent them to classes.

After school the girls talked all the way to the bus. Julie said good-by and Lynn climbed aboard with her load of books.

She transferred automatically, her mind in a maze of thoughts. When walking up her street she slowed her pace, oblivious of the cutting wind. *Lord, take over. Please don't let me fail — whatever happens at home.*

The strength came. It was good to walk up to the door with this new assurance.

Bette, in stretch pants that made her look chubby, lay on the couch among newspapers and movie magazines, chewing on a candy bar. The TV blared a commercial.

A strident voice reached her from the kitchen. "Lynn! Are you there?"

Lynn walked in with her books and faced Bernice calmly. "Yes. What can I do?"

Her stepmother, rummaging through the cupboard, glanced up at her sharply. "You'll have to run to the store for eggs. I've got to have some right away."

"All right, I'll go in a sec." Lynn was on her way down the hall to the stairs. *The quietness and assurance are mine. Thank you, Lord.*

The phone rang and Bernice yelled, "Phone, Lynn."

Carla's voice was breathlessly excited. "Lynn, I've got to talk to you a minute."

Bernice cut in, "Lynn, hang up! You've got to go!"

Lynn closed her eyes. *In quietness and confidence shall be your strength.* She covered one ear and tried to concentrate on Carla. "Go ahead, honey, I'm listening."

"Jodi called me. She came home by train because she said

Kurt wouldn't go with her and Hal and some others to another apartment. He came back Sunday afternoon. Was she mad!

"But what I want to tell you is that Craig and Tony are inseparable now. She said they were both in jail with a gang from the Village. Police raid on the weed in a dorm near Washington Square. And the police not only found roaches — you know, cig butts — they found a box of capsules and these kids were filling them with LSD! Jodi says they do it to make money. Lynn, I'm glad Kurt wasn't with them. He's been too busy with that jazz band to hang around his nutty brother's apartment."

Lynn said, "I'll pray about — " when Bernice marched over and shouted in her ear.

"I said hang up! And I mean it. Do you understand?"

Carla gasped, "Oh, oh! Bye, Lynnie," and hung up.

The tone of wrath, which usually made her limp, failed to unnerve Lynn. She faced Bernice and said quietly, "I believe God wanted me to listen to this girl for a few minutes. She was saved at retreat."

Bernice's head shot up. She opened her mouth to speak, but no words came. She moved to the table and rearranged the centerpiece.

The side door opened and Bernice fumbled in her apron pocket for a hanky. As Bert walked in whistling, she threw herself upon his shoulder whimpering, "I just don't understand it! I do everything I can to make a home and she is getting beyond me. She's obstinate — "

"That is not true, Daddy." Lynn was surprised at an inner calmness which made her voice clear and steady. She sensed her father's wonder and inwardly prayed for continued power.

"Well," he said uncertainly, "*something* is wrong. I can see that. Suppose you tell me what it's all about this time. I'll try to referee."

Lynn started to speak, but Bernice cut in, "Bert, I'm not going to put up with this another day. Either you stand by me — I'm your *wife*, you know — or I'll get a divorce. I'm not playing second fiddle to anybody, not even your daughter." She sat down at the table and let her head sag in her hands.

Lynn's heart thumped wildly. Her father's face set and she knew he was growing nervous and angry. He turned on her. "Go and study!"

Each step was agony. Her father's rejection crushed her. The feeling of guilt at being the cause of trouble between him and his wife erased God's Word from her mind. She stumbled to her room.

Too stunned to cry, she sat down at her desk and dropped her head on the stack of books. "Oh, God," she breathed, "I'll have to leave. It's getting too hard. Please let me out."

Study was impossible. During following weeks her grades slumped. Each day the storm beat down. Bernice seemed intent on shattering Lynn's new-found strength.

Bert kept busy away from home. He usually returned after Lynn was through with the dishes and was studying in her room. His coolness cut her sensitive heart and the wound grew deeper.

Early one Saturday Lynn awakened to the bitter cold of mid-January. A glance at the twin bed showed Bette a heap under her blankets. Lynn shuddered at the cheerless sight of skeleton tree arms scratching on the panes.

Then she remembered. *Today's my birthday!* She was to receive a letter from her mother's lawyer in Virginia today. But *Mother* was gone, and Dad was not the same since their move to Philadelphia. And Joel had changed.

The pressures building up wracked her soul. She broke into sobbing and covered her mouth with the quilt to hold back the sounds. *I'm going to ask Julie if she knows what's wrong. I've got to know before he goes away to college.*

The tears raining down relieved her heartache. She closed her eyes and sleep came. When she awakened, the winter sun was pouring through the room.

Her watch showed nine-thirty. She would creep downstairs and put on the coffee pot. It would be good to sit at the table alone and drink something hot while she read her Bible.

In robe and slippers she padded past the sleeping Bette,

noiselessly descended the stairs, and was in the kitchen before she realized anyone was there.

Bernice jerked back from the stove, a strange look of dismay on her face. She clasped a long white envelope in both hands. A bottle of glue fell from the edge of the counter to the floor.

15

Lynn started to pick up the bottle but Bernice snatched it. "Mind your own business!" she snapped. Then she marched through the dining room to the front hall.

The tea kettle's shrill whistle sent Lynn to turn off the stove. She called, "Shall I go ahead with breakfast?"

Bernice's answer was a brief, "Yes."

Her stepmother's actions were strange. Was she trying to conceal something? The letter! Was it *the* letter? The one her own mother had sent through their lawyer? Lynn froze. What should she do? *Lord, lead me.*

The prayer from her heart gave assurance. Quietly she moved to the hall. Bernice was reading a post card. The long letter lay on the table with other mail.

"Oh, did the mail come?" Lynn crossed the hall.

"Looks like it!" Bernice tripped upstairs.

Lynn searched the mail and read the long envelope. It was addressed to Miss Lynn Hathaway Hale from Benson and Benson in Virginia.

Her hands trembled with eagerness. Then she noticed the shiny oozing of glue from the envelope. It was still sticky! She stared in unbelief. Bernice couldn't be *that* underhanded! Yet here was evidence. And the teakettle! *She read my letter and barely had it glued shut when I came in.*

Lynn sat down at the kitchen table to read the contents.

It was a brief business letter containing a check for one thousand dollars, designated in her "deceased mother's last will and testament" for her daughter, to be used in furthering her education. Lynn bowed her head and cried. The longing for her old home swept all else from her mind.

"Well! Happy birthday, my eighteen-year-old, beautiful daughter."

She lifted her head and smiled at her father. He bent down and kissed her.

"What's this? The letter? Bernice said she opened some mail by mistake this morning, and she was afraid you would not believe her. So I told her I would explain."

Bernice swept in, her usual cocky self. "I stopped reading the minute I saw it was for you, dear," she said briskly, banging the coffee canister lid to the counter. She measured coffee into the pot. "Of course I couldn't help noticing your check. Congratulations!"

"It will really help meet expenses for my first year at Bible college next fall, won't it, Dad?"

"Well, honey, by the time you enter college in the fall we'll have our finances well in hand and I can see you through." He glanced at Bernice.

His pause sent a thrill of apprehension through Lynn. Her stepmother's breezy entrance held meaning this morning. Bernice had already talked to her father about this check!

"What he is trying to say is what I've tried to get across to you for a long time, Lynn. You are part of a new family, my dear. You never would have had a sister if it hadn't been for your father's marriage to me."

Lynn's intuition relayed the message: *Bernice wants me to share this money with Bette!*

"Dad," she said evenly, "Mother's will stated that this was for my college expenses. It will save you a lot next fall, and I'd much rather have it that way."

Bernice covered her eyes with a hanky. "She never will accept us, Bert. She's never entered the family — just keeps herself aloof — and I've tried so hard!"

Her stepmother's false sorrow closed the case. Lynn

folded the check into the envelope and walked to the door without looking back.

The pressure of past months clamped down like a giant hand. Lynn found it hard to hold up her head. She was so tired — so terribly tired. She closed the bathroom door behind her, ran cold water, and bathed her face.

Something was going on outside the door. She held her breath to listen. A strange low tone from Bernice: ". . . had enough, Bert Hale! . . . protected your big overgrown baby for the last time! . . . time she did go! . . . I'll get a divorce . . ."

It's time she did go. Lynn sank to her knees by the bathtub and leaned her head on her arms. It was impossible to stay on after this. Her father's voice rose in frenzied pitch. "Lynn, since you want to be so independent, you can support yourself. Understand?"

Yes, dear God. I do understand. This was the time to leave. Her father might have some peace in the family if she was not here. It was quite clear now that she was the main cause of all the friction. The assurance that flooded her soul gave Lynn physical strength. Her legs were no longer weak as she stood and crossed to the door.

His fist banged on the door as she opened it. She had never seen her father like this. A white line seemed drawn around his mouth, as he clenched and unclenched his fists.

Bernice stood at the top of the stairs, head cocked to one side in the attitude Lynn knew so well. Lynn felt a sudden surge of relief at the prospect of leaving all this behind.

Bette bellowed from the bedroom, "Will you shut up out there. I can't sleep!"

Lynn spoke softly, "I'm sorry that I've seemed ungrateful. God knows my heart and He knows yours." As their eyes met, Bernice's narrowed to slits. Lynn went on. "If you two really needed the money, I'd give it *all* to you gladly, but — "

Bernice laughed harshly. Bert turned on his heel and stomped downstairs; Bernice followed.

Lynn hesitated before entering her room. Where was her old suitcase? She would have to pack her things. Bette kept her head covered and Lynn moved about quietly. Her belongings from the loaded desk, dresser drawers, and closet shelves would have to be sorted and packed.

She began to sort clothing into neat stacks on her bed. A car door slammed. Where was her father going? Or was it Bernice? She looked out and caught a glimpse of the car as it backed from the driveway. Both! Bernice and her father were going somewhere. That was strange.

Mechanically Lynn returned to the kitchen and poured a cup of coffee. Time was slipping by; she began to panic. What should she do? Where could she go? She gathered newspapers from the living room and searched the ads. There were columns of addresses but only one or two rooms for rent in the Howard High district. Maybe she should talk with Sherry. Her neighborhood was between school and church.

Miss Lindy! Why hadn't she thought of her before? Nervously Lynn dialed the phone.

"Yes?"

"Miss Lindy — " Lynn's voice broke. She paused a minute to recover.

"What is wrong, Lynn? This *is* Lynn, isn't it?"

"Yes. I must see you. The time has come. I can't stay here — not even today. My stepmother threatened divorce — and all on account of me."

"You come right over, dear. I'll be here all day and you are more than welcome to stay overnight."

Lynn placed the phone with a sigh of relief. Then she flew into action. The break had come, and she must move quickly before they could stop her.

She ran to the basement and sorted clothing in the basket, stuffing her things in one of her own blue pillow slips. She would keep her pair of blue sheets and make up the bed with some of Bernice's from the hall closet. *But I can't stay at Miss Lindy's very long.*

Sherry again came to mind. Lynn dialed her number and Sherry answered with a yawn, "Yeah? What's with you at this unearthly hour! Don't you know it's Saturday — the only day of the week I can sleep in?"

"Listen, kid! I'm in real trouble; I have to leave home!" Sherry came to life and Lynn went on, "Please try to think

— where can I move today. Yes, *today!*" Lynn explained as briefly as she could. "Oh, thank you, Sherry. I knew you were like that. And Sherry, please don't tell Julie about this yet."

Sherry said, "I get you. Wasn't that something what her mother said about Joel's future relationship with girls? Julie said Joel looked baffled. Why, kid, I wouldn't have thought Evans's were that type — sort of snooty, if you ask me! A girl with 'background similar to his!' As though you weren't quite up to his level! Boy! How do you like that?"

The shock took Lynn's breath away. *So that was it.* The mystery was solved. No wonder Joel's attitude toward her had changed. His parents accepted her as a friend of the family but had no desire to see her become a member of it. Joel would be looking for someone else. *Someone else.* She stared across the room while Sherry chatted on.

Then she remembered. "Sherry, I've got to go. The folks might come back any minute. Oh, do help me think what to do!"

Lynn rummaged in the basement. She found the box she needed and packed her belongings without disturbing Bette. An hour passed and her parents had not returned. Lynn prayed in whispers, "Lord, help! Show me what to do — now!"

The phone rang and she was surprised to hear Mrs. Stone's musical voice. "Hello, my darling. Guess what already! Your girl friend, Sherry, is calling me. She is telling me you are looking for a room.

"Leen, I am telling you what. Gil is going to the university next week. You are coming here. You are packing your things and — no, no, I don't want you should say one word. We understand already. Look! Gil is wanting that he should go to this university in New York. Oy, I am missing that boy already!

"So we want you should come here until school is out. After that — we see what gives. Now don't say another word. You are coming by us and it won't cost you a cent for his room. Leen, we are so lonesome already — only one son and one grandson — we never had a daughter, Leen. We need a daughter."

82

Lynn was stunned. "I don't know what to say, Mrs. Stone. You are so kind, so very kind. Yes, I'm sure I can stay with friends for a few days until Gil leaves. How can I ever thank you — "

"We are thanking *you*, darling. Sherry is telling me she knows from the Evans girl what we said — that we are missing our grandson. She is right away thinking of you and we want you should move your things here this morning. Gil and a boy friend are here and they are coming over to pick up your things. You are having lunch with us. From here we talk. So you are packing your suitcase and the boys will be right over. Yah?"

"Well — I was praying all morning and this must be the answer. It must be!"

"Of course it is, darling. Don't cry. Just come. You are doing us a favor, believe me. Now you get ready. Gil and David are coming over."

Mrs. Stone hung up and Lynn looked blankly at the phone. Then a wave of relief thrilled her. She whirled around the kitchen in an ecstasy of freedom. "I feel like Hansel and Gretel when they got away from — oh! What am I saying?"

Gil was right about his family: *"you'll never meet better people in this world."* After the harsh words and cruel coldness in this house, Mrs. Stone's warm welcome sounded like *home*.

Quietness and confidence. The twin promises of God were like wings lifting her above storm clouds. Bless Miss Lindy. Her faithful testimony helped today. Lynn started to gather coats from the hall closet. She had better carry a few loads downstairs before the boys arrived. What would happen if her folks drove in at the same time? She dashed upstairs, went to work, and had all but the big box carried to the front door when the boys arrived.

Gil said, "Hello, Lynn. Good to see you. Here's my friend David." And they went to work. His voice was so kind — as though he knew her trouble. "Is this all?" He looked around.

"Oh! No, there is one more box — a large one — in my room." Lynn ran ahead.

Bette emerged from her nest squawking, "What are you *doing*, Lynn Hale!"

"I'm moving out, Bette."

"Who's coming?" Bette heard the boys' voices and bolted for the bathroom seconds before Gil came up.

It took only a few minutes. Lynn checked the closet and dresser carefully to make sure she had not left anything behind. Then she threw her coat around her shoulders, grabbed her stack of books, and followed the boys to the car.

16

As THEY BACKED FROM THE DRIVE, it hit her. She was actually leaving her father's house. She tried to hold back the tears.

Gil seemed to understand. "Lynn, from what I've heard about your stepmother, I think you are wise to make this move. David's father is a lawyer, and if you need any legal advice —"

"Oh, I do! I do right now. But it isn't possible — I suppose on Saturday he wouldn't —"

David said, "I'll phone from Gil's house. He's a great guy and he'll understand. Won't cost you a penny, either. You ask him anything you like. I'll explain first, and then you can talk with him."

Lynn felt the burden lifting. "Thank God," she said softly. "Oh, Gil, God has led in this today. I didn't know where to turn. And the folks are *never* away Saturday mornings. Yet they went somewhere just long enough for me to move my things. I can't tell you how embarrassing it would have been for you if my stepmother had been home. The neighbors have —"

When Lynn stopped, her face flaming, Gil said quickly, "That's what I meant, Lynn. I've heard all about it. Rosenfelds from our temple live three doors from your house.

Word gets around. So don't worry how we feel about it. The whole Jewish community will take you in, even as my saufa has."

"Your what?"

David smiled back at her. "That's Jewish for 'Grandmother.' I have a sawv and a saufa too — sawv meaning grandfather in Hebrew."

Lynn said shyly, "Jewish family life must be wonderful. But I don't want you to think all Christian homes are like this."

Gil laughed. "We could show you some Jewish homes that we aren't proud of. And others that are ideal, as you say, so — "

"So it's the same everywhere. Here's our corner, Gil." David shrugged his shoulders expressively.

Lynn started to say, "I'll gladly pay for — " but the boys looked shocked and hurt.

"What are friends for?" they told her.

David opened her door and reached for her armload of books. Mrs. Stone was right there, ready to clasp her in a warm embrace. Lynn broke down from the strain of the past hours.

That evening she sat in Miss Lindy's tiny kitchen and told her what had happened. "God took care of me and I'll never forget it, Miss Lindy. I've told you how it worked those last days in my stepmother's house — the assurance He gave me — and how it became clear that I should separate from them. And God took care of the next steps.

"I talked with the lawyer and then he talked to Mrs. Stone. He told her what he warned me about. I am not to talk to either my father or Bernice about that money. The lawyer asked for my pastor's name and phone number. I wonder why?

"So Mrs. Stone answered the phone each time it rang and Dad called in the afternoon. I heard her say, 'Yes, she is here and you are not coming over to see her. We have a lawyer who is taking care of her business, and I would be advising your wife to stay away from my house. What she has done to this poor girl shouldn't happen to a dog.' This

85

embarrassed me, Miss Lindy, but it is just the way these people talk — and I couldn't help it, of course."

"This also is allowed by our Father in heaven for some purpose." Miss Lindy was serene. She poured hot chocolate into fragile blue and white cups and set cookies on the table. "Now let's thank Him for His lovingkindness to us."

As her teacher prayed, Lynn knew a moment of utter peace. Severing from her former life had taken place so quickly that the wound was clean. There seemed no jagged edges except — *Joel!* Even as Miss Lindy prayed, Lynn was thinking: *He'll be looking for someone else. Someone else. Even he doesn't care!*

"Lynn, my dear girl, you are quite worn out. I'll fix your bed on the davenport right away."

Lynn lifted her head. "I'm tired, but it helps to talk to you. Are you sure it won't disturb you — having me here for a week?"

Miss Lindy reached across the little table to pat her hand. "Now don't you fret about it for one minute. I count this a privilege. It is actually an answer to my prayers, for I asked God to make me of some special blessing in your life."

"Dear Miss Lindy, you have already been a big blessing to me."

"Lynn, are you sure you should make your home with these Jewish people for the rest of your school term? That will be at least five months, won't it?"

"It would be impossible to refuse their hospitality. You'll have to meet Eemah. She asked me to call her that. It's Hebrew for mother. Isn't that lovely of her? Yes, I'm sure the Lord has led me there. The way He opened the door this morning — it was a miracle!"

"The waters of the Red Sea parted and God's people walked through," observed Miss Lindy. "He is a God of miracles. We'll pray that He will reach the hearts of this precious couple through you, Lynn, and that their eyes may be opened to the Light of the world, their own Hebrew Messiah and Redeemer of Israel."

"And you should see the lovely room I'll have. It's Gil's room, and I've already told them I'll stay with a girl friend any weekend he wants to come home from college, so he can be with his family. Mrs. Stone — I mean Eemah — told me she loved me like a daughter already yet." Lynn's dimples came through. "I'm beginning to talk like they do."

The phone rang and they both started. Lynn's heart thumped.

Miss Lindy answered, "Hello? Mrs. Stone. No, she is right here. She'll speak to you."

Lynn lifted the receiver. "Eemah? He did? He will? Oh, thank you, Mrs. Stone."

Miss Lindy said, "Your father?"

"Yes. He's going to call me here. Oh, dear! This is it!"

On the third ring Miss Lindy was prepared to answer. "Hello?"

Lynn stood by, pressing her hands together. The old ache crept into her throat and tightened like a vise around her heart. Her lips were white and straight.

Miss Lindy looked at her and said into the phone, "Mr. Hale, I know you have had a harrowing day, but you do not seem to realize your daughter's condition after *her* ordeal. I suggest you talk to her on the phone tonight instead. Then you may see her tomorrow at church. It is time for me to retire and I would really appreciate — yes? All right, sir. Here she is."

His voice was strained, almost hoarse. "Young lady, you have caused your family enough embarrassment for one day. Now you get your things packed by tomorrow, because after church I'm coming after you. Understand?"

Lynn closed her eyes. *Help, Lord.* She lost her breath. "Dad — "

"Speak up so I can hear you!"

"I can't come back there to live. If I had to come back, I wouldn't be well enough to continue school. You don't understand how she is when you're not home. She's two different people. I'm sure you will all get along better without me — "

"Lynn — "

He seemed at a loss for words. Lynn said, "It's far better this way. I'm sure God will help you see it as He has shown me the past few weeks and today especially. Daddy, we can visit each other. It isn't as though — "

87

"We'll talk about it tomorrow. I'm so tired I can't think."

Lynn felt weak. She replaced the receiver shakily and turned to find Miss Lindy sitting with head bowed in prayer.

"It's going to be all right, isn't it, my dear?" The little lady's sprightly manner brought back some color to Lynn's lips.

"Yes, it has to be."

Sunday they awoke to a snowstorm. Miss Lindy's house was planted between brick sidewalks and alley among other small houses in a long row. The white doors with brass knockers looked like a series of Christmas card pictures.

"I love your little house, Miss Lindy. Sherry calls it a dollhouse."

"It's patterned like the Betsy Ross house, but we have more room than she did. Three rooms down and the large attic upstairs which could easily be converted into a bedroom. My neighbor's two children have a lovely large room upstairs."

Lynn looked out the window. "They are outside shoveling snow. Let me take your broom and sweep the doorstep."

The front door opened on the sidewalk. Little white window boxes down the street were mounded over with snow frostings. The storm would soon blow drifts against the doors. Lynn swept hard, but the strong wind blew gales of snow into her face. She gave up and went inside.

"It's a bad storm, Miss Lindy. Good thing you live close to church."

"I'm so glad you are here today, Lynn. I'll have someone's arm to hold."

Lynn's heart went out to the little lady. Brave little saint living alone with sad memories of faded hopes. But this lady had discovered the way of gladness. She did not carry the burden of sadness upon her. Lynn loved the way Miss Lindy's black eyes twinkled with the joy of life. *Could I be this joyful if Joel leaves me?* Lynn could not comprehend such a possibility.

She helped Miss Lindy into her red wool coat. They each tied wool scarves on their heads.

Around the corner they met Carla, bent against the wind,

Bible under her arm. Lynn dreaded the ordeal of explaining. Carla walked with them, taking Lynn's presence for granted.

When they entered the church doors and removed their scarves, she showed surprise. "You came with Miss Lindy."

Lynn nodded.

"Well — "

"I stayed at her house last night, Carla."

"Oh."

They took their usual seats in the senior high department. Sherry's entrance was punctuated with her usual witty comments.

After the singing and announcements the girls moved through the crowded hall to their classroom. Carla said, "I'm waiting for Julie. She's late today, and I want to tell you girls about Jodi."

They gathered in a clump to listen. "Jodi wanted me to come over Friday night — even came after me — and guess why! Tony and Hal were there waiting. Tony wanted me to join 'em for a big blast in this millionaire's fabulous layout on the Hudson. Then do you know what! Craig blew in. He called me a dope and worse things than that and — wait! Here she comes. Julie, sit by me."

In class Carla told the rest. "Miss Lindy, did I say this right? Craig was mad at me and made a sarcastic remark about perfumed polecats. He said it would take an opera-tion to remove the 'scent' from this old sinner.

"And I said, 'You're so right. It did take an operation of the Holy Spirit to remove the old desires and turn me toward God.' I told him I was a sinner all right, but saved by God's grace."

"Good for you! You couldn't have said it better. Now shall we keep praying definitely for these young people mentioned, girls? And before we bow in prayer, are there any other prayer requests this morning? Yes, I know one unspoken request." She saw Lynn's gesture.

Lynn felt Julie's long searching gaze, but kept her eyes on their teacher. After class she walked ahead, but Julie hurried to catch up. She sounded impatient. "Aren't you going to *tell* me about it? How could you move to Stones

— of all people — Lynn? You could at least have talked over your — your problems — with my mother first."

Lynn met Julie's eyes calmly. "I have a feeling that your mother would not have understood my problem, Julie."

Julie walked with her to the sanctuary. Lynn knew why she had no answer.

17

JULIE LEFT TO SING in the choir, and Lynn waited for Sherry and Carla. She need not look for Joel; the last few Sundays he had avoided her. And she had been so blind. *Oh, Joel, Joel! If you really cared — as you told me so many times — you could never change.*

Where was her father? Was he also going to avoid her? It might be easier that way.

The pastor's wife slipped over to say softly, "Lynn, we are praying for you. We understand. Call us any time, dear."

Quick tears blinded Lynn's vision. She said a fervent, "Thank you." Then a group of girls surrounded her.

When they were seated, one whispered loudly, "Lynn Hale! What's this I hear about you?"

From the conversation buzzing around, Lynn gathered that the story was all through the congregation. It seemed one of Pauline's friends had driven by her house at the time Gil and David were hauling her things to the car. They must have seen her get in the car with "those strange boys." Then they probably called her folks to report and get more information. She could imagine what Bernice had said and how she said it.

When Joel stayed away from her after the service, Lynn's bitter cup was full.

In the afternoon when she started to cough and run a slight temperature, Miss Lindy said, "Lynn, you stay right

90

on that couch through Monday. I'm going to fix you some hot ginger for that cough."

Lynn rested with her head on two large pillows, feeling the reaction from yesterday's siege. She was too weak to sit up.

Miss Lindy brought her a steaming cup of hot milk with honey and ginger. It burned Lynn's throat with each swallow, but tasted good and checked the cough.

Miss Lindy sat in a rocker and looked out at the white swirl. "It's turning to sleet," she said. "Well, my dear little friend, your folks can't touch you *or* the money. I am truly amazed at the way the Lord took care of you — even supplying the services of a good lawyer free of charge."

"I wondered why he asked the name of my pastor?" Lynn curled her feet up under the quilt and closed her eyes.

"From what Pastor told you," said Miss Lindy, "I believe he has had a long talk with your lawyer about the whole business. Now you roll this whole burden on the Lord. I'm going into my room to take a nap, and you rest. Hear?"

It was heavenly to lie still and rest. The peace of this godly home, small as it was, restored Lynn's soul.

She prayed inwardly, "Dear Lord, let me have a little home like this some day — with Joel — if it be Thy will. I don't care about a fine home like most people want . . ."

"Lynn, you slept right through until morning. My dear girl, you must have been exhausted. How do you feel?"

Lynn emerged from her quilt. "I haven't slept this soundly through the night since I left Virginia. Miss Lindy, your little home is a heaven on earth. I wish I could live here always. Oh, dear! My exams!" She jumped up, then sat down quickly and held her head in her hands.

Miss Lindy nodded. "You stay in bed today, Lynn. You are suffering battle fatigue. Spiritual warfare is even harder on a person than physical. Lynn, you have fought with powers of evil and God has given you the victory, but that does not mean you can snap back in a few hours. You need a rest.

"And how thankful I am to our wonderful heavenly

Father that He sent you to me. I am enjoying every moment of your stay."

That afternoon Carla blew in after school. "Thought Lynn would like me to bring her tomorrow's assignments. Brother! Exams start Wednesday!" She collapsed in a red plush chair by the window. "Cute little place you have here, Miss Lindy."

Miss Lindy poured a glass of orange juice and handed a tray to Carla.

"You're great!" Carla held up a large sugar cookie. "Just what I need! Getting fatter by the furlong, as Kurt would say."

Lynn saw the tremble of her chin as she lifted her glass. The girl missed her friends. Lynn said, "Let's meet at the bus tomorrow. I won't know where to transfer."

"Don't haveta. Only two miles to school straight as the crow flaps from here. Boy! I'll be glad to have someone to ride with. Jodi dropped me since — "

"Since you were saved, Carla?"

"Yeah. But I'm not missing anything, Miss Lindy. Ya know, Lynn? Three of our friends are graduating this Friday night: Joel Evans, Gil Stone, and Jodi."

Carla continued. "Lynn, Kurt asked about ya today at lunch. He said he didn't blame you one bit for moving away from home. Said his mother wasn't surprised either. Wonder why? Did *she* know anything about your stepmother?"

A scene from Kathy's Cafe flashed in Lynn's memory. "A little," she said, looking down at her glass.

Carla continued, "I can't understand Julie Evans! She — of all people — doesn't think you did right. I don't get it. And she's your best friend!"

Miss Lindy smiled, "Your *best* friend, Carla?"

Carla looked blank. Then she slapped a hand over her mouth and laughed. "And you just talked about it yesterday in class! How soon can I forget? Well, of course our Lord is your best friend, Lynn."

Lynn kept looking at her glass. "I know what you mean. But the Evans' family, I think, are rather smug at times. They are a good example of the 'pious attitude of past centuries' we've been studying in sociology."

The bitter undertone did not escape Miss Lindy. She mentally catalogued Lynn's statements for future reference.

Carla was quick. "Well, kid, ya can't win 'em all. You've got me, the old goulash gal from the wrong side of town. Oops! Miss Lindy! I didn't mean – oh, my! What I mean is – "

Their teacher threw back her head and laughed. The girls soon joined her. Miss Lindy wiped her eyes with her apron. "Our side of town is the best side, isn't is, Carla? I wouldn't think of living any other place. You couldn't find better neighbors in the whole city."

Lynn sighed, "I know why you are such a wonderful Christian. You practice what you preach. 'Godliness with contentment is great gain.'"

"I wish my mom would learn that!" Carla carried her tray to the sink and rinsed her glass under the faucet. "She keeps nagging my poor dad about the bills and how she does ironing for people. And all the time he's holding down two different jobs to keep us afloat, and she can't see that he's killing himself.

"When he's gone, she'll miss him, or at least she'll miss the dollars he brings home and slaps on the table. Hands 'em all over because he knows she'll buy groceries. All he buys is beer. Whatta life!"

The room was still a moment. Carla went on, "But I've found the answer. 'I've discovered the way of gladness.' I love that song they sang at retreat. Miss Lindy, please keep praying for Kurt and Jodi and Craig Barr. Those kids think they're having fun, and they don't care that they're gambling with their lives – their souls – only they don't know it."

"I am praying for each of you every day, Carla."

As the week went by, Lynn and Carla became closer friends. They rode the bus each day, and Carla took Lynn home after school to meet her mother, a pudgy woman who wore a ribbon bow above frizzy dyed bangs. Mrs. Kumarek fussed over Carla a lot, and Lynn could see that the woman adored her daughter.

Carla said later, "I wish my mom wouldn't descend on me like that – the minute I walk in. She bugs me!"

Lynn thought awhile. Carla said, "What's the matter?"

93

Lynn replied, "It's better to have someone who loves you fussing *over* you than to have someone who doesn't care for you making a fuss *about* you."

"Aw, Lynn! Honestly, kid, I didn't mean to hit a sore spot. I'm sorry!"

"It's okay, Carla."

During the week Mrs. Stone called about the celebration. It was to be on Saturday night before Gil left town. She said, "Leen, darling, I want you should come home to live with us this coming Sunday. And I have asked your girl friend, Julie, to pick you up on Saturday night already and bring you out to the open-house we are having for Gil's friends to be celebrating his graduation.

"You can't come? Nonsense! Of course you come. You are mine *daughter*, remember? Look! Gil's father is here from Europe already and he is driving his son to New York with all the luggage.

"Oy, it is being so lonesome, Leen. I can't tell you how much we are loving that boy! He is such a good boy. I love him as my own son. I am going now, darling. And you come Saturday night."

Lynn told Carla about it on the way to school. "They wouldn't understand if I stayed away. And I don't want to go!"

"Stop worrying about the Evans family. You haven't done anything wrong. Just because they don't happen to understand it. Why, Lynn, how can people judge each other from what they see? You are the one who *knows* how it was."

"Yes, but Mrs. Evans would trust Bernice's word against mine. I'm merely a 'temperamental teen-ager' as far as she knows."

"All right, Lynn Hale. I'm gonna pray about it. I'll pray that God will show Mrs. Evans who is right and show Joel, too. He's the dumbest guy I ever saw, and I don't think much of him for letting you down like he has. If I were you, I'd write him right out of my little book!"

18

Lynn dreaded Saturday evening. She couldn't accept a ride from Joel. "What shall I do?" she asked Miss Lindy.

"You could take a bus and go early. Maybe Mrs. Stone could use some extra help."

Lynn brushed a kiss on the velvet creek. "Thank you. That is exactly what I'll do."

Mrs. Stone was thrilled to see her. Lynn helped her arrange the cakes on silver trays which gleamed on a mahogany table. They lighted candles as guests began to arrive.

Lynn was surrounded by Stones' Jewish friends, when she heard familiar voices. Her heart pumped a fast beat. She glanced in the wall mirror over the massive buffet and met her own frightened eyes. *In quietness and confidence shall be your strength.* God's promise crossed her mind. Instantly she noticed a change in her own reflection. The pink cheeks still matched the yarn roses in her navy wool dress, but her expression was clear. She would meet them in the strength of the One she trusted. *Dear Lord, keep me from trembling when I see them.*

Several minutes passed before the group surrounding her scattered and guests began filing past the table. Lynn poured coffee at one end of the buffet. When Mrs. Evans approached, she seemed cheerful, "Well, Lynn! I'm surprised to see you here."

Lynn smiled, but did not trust herself to speak.

Mr. Evans was as cordial as ever. "Hello, my dear. Imagine — whipped cream for my coffee! Mrs. Stone tells me it is delicious. Aren't the Stones a charming couple?"

Lynn shared his mood. "I love them."

Mr. Evans bent his head to whisper, "Who knows whether

you are come — like Esther — 'for such a time as this.' God has a plan, I'm sure."

Lynn relaxed until Joel passed with his plate of cakes and punch. His expression, far from cold, held uncertainty, a slight dash of compassion, and some element of love. He paused and kept watching her as she tried to concentrate on the next person in line.

Then he spoke, "May I take you to Miss Lindy's afterwards?"

She shot a quick look of surprise. "Why, I guess so."

She nodded absently and answered someone's questions about the cream pitcher.

Julie was next, talking with Kurt's mother. They introduced Lynn to Mr. Chase, a handsome man, even taller than Kurt.

Mrs. Stone asked her to come and have some cookies with the others in the front room.

Lynn chose a chair in a corner of the dining room, but Mrs. Stone called, "Leen, darling, come here. This is my new daughter, Rabbi. Isn't she a darling!"

Lynn wished she could disappear. The gleam of interest she caught in Mrs. Evans' eye irritated her.

The rabbi and his wife welcomed her warmly. The Jewish folk were all, as Eemah said, wonderful people.

Finally the evening came to an end. Lynn kissed Eemah good-night with a promise to be back the next day. Joel held her coat, and Mrs. Stone called from the door, "You take good care of my daughter!"

"I will," he said cheerfully.

But when he closed the car door, after climbing in beside her, Lynn felt a chill of formality descend.

He drove several blocks silently. Then, "Lynn, I don't quite know how to say this but — well, I'm sure I owe it to you."

"You don't owe me a thing, Joel." She guessed his motive and turned cold. She knew he caught the inflection of hardness; there was nothing tender in her tone.

His own manner changed abruptly. He pulled to the curb. "Lynn, I must confess that my feeling for you has never changed. I *care*. It's just that — "

96

In his pause she was tempted to say *"but your mother thinks I am not good enough for you."* She bit her tongue.

He covered her hand with his; she jerked away and looked out the window.

"What I'm trying to say is that I really don't think it is fair to *you* to feel obligated to me. You should feel absolutely free to date others — "

"Feel obligated! If it has come to *that*, we'll call it quits, Joel. I know what you are trying to say. So go right ahead. Date other girls! There's no doubt about it — you'll meet someone else who will be the 'perfect mate.' Well, maybe I will too. I'd like to go now. It's getting late."

In the night she tossed restlessly. Why did she have to be so bitter about it? She had acted like a child.

Philadelphia without Joel was a cardboard city with papier-mache people. Lynn accompanied Eemah to social affairs at the Jewish center and various homes. She went through all the motions, but her heart wasn't in it.

For several weekends Gil came home, and Lynn spent weekends with Carla or Miss Lindy.

Carla's mother was delighted to have her. She explained, "Carla needs friends. I kept asking her — where are the girls you talked so much about?" Lynn's thoughts were bitter. *The girls are in smug little cliques.*

Lynn shared Carla's room. They studied together and shared confidences. As weeks brought spring nearer, Lynn confided in Carla. "Julie comes to see me like you do — she loves the Stones — and Eemah invites her to dinner as she does you, but we aren't like we used to be. She's friendly, but I've lost her for a friend."

Carla clamped her shoulders in a bear hug. "Honey, I'm still praying that something will reveal the truth. Lynn, I needed a Christian friend. You know I'm not the type to run around by myself. And if this misunderstanding hadn't come between you and Julie, I'll bet you wouldn't have been slum — I mean — chumming around with the likes o' me. And maybe I wouldn't have gone so far with the Lord. It's selfish of me, but I'm sorta glad you felt some loneliness like I did."

Suddenly Lynn understood. She threw her arms around Carla. "We're in the same boat," she said.

Carla leaned her head on Lynn's shoulder. "Yep, it's sink or swim, mate."

Lynn began to sink when Joel brought a strange girl to church on Easter Sunday.

The day began with a glowing red sunrise. Lynn had slept at Carla's so they could walk together in the early dawn to the annual Easter breakfast.

Lynn hummed *He Lives* all the way to church. Carla was excited; her parents had promised to meet her for morning worship service at eleven. "What a wonderful day! And to think — no school for a solid week!"

Lynn was radiant. "I am just as thrilled as you are. Gil's folks are coming to church with Evans's. You know Gil and Joel have been seeing each other quite often, Julie tells me. It seems they meet at a city library and Gil has begun asking questions about the Bible.

"Julie says Joel believes Gil is seriously comparing the Old and New Testaments. Places like the twenty-second Psalm which foretold Christ's sufferings and His exact words on the cross hundreds of years before it actually happened!"

"Lynn Hale! It looks to me like *you* have been studying!"

"I only looked into it because Julie got us interested. She reads parts like that to Eemah and Mr. Stone when she comes over about once a week. She's trying to get them to see that Christ Jesus is the Messiah and their Passover Lamb."

Then they saw her. A tall girl beside Joel — slightly taller than he, honey blond — walking beside him from the parking lot to the side door.

Lynn, who was humming, stopped in the middle of a note and grasped Carla's arm.

Carla said, "Don't panic. Could be a cousin visiting the family."

They stepped inside and both stopped short.

Halfway downstairs a group of young people were gathered around Joel. His voice carried clearly, "Natalie Worthington is the daughter of an old schoolmate of my father's, a doctor of science who is a close friend of our Dr. Winkelman."

Carla's arm circled Lynn. They both shrank into the shadows of the hall. Carla brushed tears from her own eyes. "Kid — "

"There's nothing to say, Carla. So don't try."

"Don't let it throw ya, honey. Oh, I hate boys. They're all alike — fickle — I *hate* — "

Sherry blew in and backed into them as others crowded in the doorway. "Excuse — why, Lynn! Carla! Hi!"

Sherry took a second look. "What's the matter with you two?" She lowered her voice. "Anything wrong?"

Carla's black eyebrows met. "Plenty! That dumb Joel oughta have his head cracked open. And if I were a boy, I'd gladly do it! Look at him down there — his arm around that girl!"

Sherry cried, "We'll stay with you, Lynn. Let's go down and find a seat as far from *them* as we can."

Lynn, white-faced, felt scalding tears racing to the surface. "You go down — save me a seat — let me have a little time alone and I'll be all right."

Carla looked doubtful, but Lynn edged toward the upper hall rest room and waved them on. She sank into a chair and put her head down. Nausea knotted her stomach. *This is it. He has someone else. I am nothing to him — nothing!*

She tried to gain strength to return to the girls, but her head began to pound. She thought of her father. He never called her and never spoke to her. It was too much to bear. She wasn't worth their time. The ones she loved the most — Dad, Joel, and Julie — didn't care whether she lived or died. Carla and Sherry could get along fine without her.

Suddenly Lynn couldn't stand it a minute longer. She had to get away from them all. She ran outside and down the street.

The warm spring morning which earlier had thrilled her soul had lost its glory. A row of yellow and orchid crocuses caught her attention. They belonged in another world.

There is no one — no one on earth who belongs to me — who really cares — no one.

The bus trip to Virginia shouldn't cost as much as train

99

fare. She would visit Aunt May during spring vacation. Spring in the Blue Ridge!

She walked slowly; the curving paths were free of cars. Here and there dogs led apartment dwellers in circles. A magnolia tree tossed pink bouquets her way; they were a part of her childhood. The familiar fragrance proclaimed: *It's Easter. He lives! He lives! Christ Jesus lives today! I see His hand of mercy. I hear His voice of cheer. Just the time I need Him, He's always near.*

19

LYNN LEANED AGAINST A TREE, shivering. She should go back to church; they were expecting her. *I can't! I won't go back!* She moved slowly along the familiar path, seeing herself and Joel as on a movie screen; they rode by smiling into each other's eyes. She felt the radiance of his special look — the one that told her she was the only one he loved. She thrilled to his handclasp. He told her how much he cared; her eyes met his with her heart's answer.

Then the vision blurred; a honey blond girl was in Joel's arms. *Oh, God, help me! I'm afraid I'll crack up.*

Lynn forced herself to look around with seeing eyes. The parkway led to main streets. She would find a restaurant and order coffee. It would take up more time and keep her steady on the long ride south; she would be traveling until almost dark.

Monday afternoon she strolled up Magnolia Hill. If only Dad had not sold the old house! It looked exactly the same except for the curtains. Her mother's white sheer ones were exchanged for red draperies. Lynn changed her mind about knocking and turned back.

The small town was different somehow. It didn't feel natural to be here. She sat down in the warm sunshine on the back step of Aunt May's tiny yellow house.

How deathly still! No rumble of traffic. Nothing to do.

Her heartbeat echoed in the silence.

Lynn picked a tall blade of grass and bit the tender green part. It would be a relief to go berry picking as her aunt suggested. But what would they do all evening? The coming week loomed ahead — a mountain of minutes to be ticked off one by one. *I can't stay here all week.*

What were the girls doing in the city? Carla would get her post card tomorrow. Eemah would have read her note Sunday noon, and the girls would hear about her visiting the hometown.

Joel would spend some time with Gil. Probably the girl was at the Evans' home for a few days. She and Julie would become friends. Natalie Worthington. The name fit. The name Evans meant money — prestige. Natalie would fit the image they had for their son. She might as well forget Joel. *I'll even change churches. I won't go back there.*

Tuesday morning Lynn faced a long day. It was too quiet here; she would see about a return bus. Aunt May said, "You just flit like a humming bird. Well, child, you're welcome to come any time, but there's not much goin' on in this town for a pretty young thing like you.

"Your school chum, Annalee, quit school last year and got married. Nothin' else to do — no money for college — couldn't leave town — " her voice trailed off. She looked absently across the yard for a minute. Then, "Yes, Lynnie, child, you're better off in the big city. I'm mighty proud to hear you're goin' to Bible school in the fall. Your mother's dying wish is granted. You received the money she laid by? Good.

"Your father fell heir to the rest of the estate when she died. Then, as you know, he sold your place on Magnolia Hill, so he came out right good. But I never did cotton to that gabby woman he picked up with — maybe she's all right but — " her voice grew weaker.

"I get the picture, auntie. Now let me help you shell those peas." Lynn was glad she had come back home, if only to get this one piece of news. Her father had never once mentioned his part of the estate. Bernice was bookkeeper, no doubt, which accounted for his silence on the subject.

Her aunt took the peas to the kitchen and Lynn carried the bag of pods to the back fence. A car rolled slowly around the corner, a sleek yellow with shiny black top. It rounded the corner and pulled up in their driveway.

A tall fellow stepped out and called, "Anybody home?"

"Kurt Chase!" Lynn's heart leaped. It was so good to see him.

He cocked his head to one side and said, "How d'ya like that! My best girl friend — and she takes off for Timbuktu without even saying good-by!" He clasped her in a bear hug.

His warmth was a tremendous comfort. Lynn fought sudden tears. Then she was aware of the others — Mrs. Chase in front and someone else.

"Oh, yes. You remember this frilly fem in the back, I'm sure. And my mother — "

The door flew wide and she was met with shouts of "Surprise!" as Sherry jumped out. They were taking a tour down the Blue Ridge Parkway to "break in Mrs. Chase's new car." Would she care to join them? They would arrive in Philly late next evening.

Lynn hoped her relief was not too apparent as she hurried to get ready. Aunt May seemed happy to meet her friends. They assured her she needn't prepare a lunch and were soon rolling south along the scenic highway.

Mrs. Chase proved good company. Sherry said, "Kurt's mother is as funny as he is."

Kurt called over his shoulder, "Get your cameras cocked. We're creeping up the skyway and you'll soon have a marvelous view of the valleys."

Mrs. Chase commented on the sights, and Sherry whispered, "Lynn! We were all simply wild wondering about you. It's a good thing you left that note for Mrs. Stone. Of course *they* thought you suddenly got homesick, and were glad you could visit your aunt. But *we* were worried; we knew better."

Lynn mumbled, "I'm sorry. Couldn't help it."

"I know, silly. Why d'ya suppose we came to the rescue? We loves ya!"

Lynn squeezed her hand. The trip with friends through her familiar territory melted the memories and the short vacation did its work. She would be glad to return to the life and routine she knew.

On the return trip Sherry observed, "You are getting relaxed now, Lynn. That dimple in your cheek comes and goes like it did. Boy! You don't know how we missed you those forty-eight hours!"

If Mrs. Chase knew why Lynn had left town, she did not ask about it. She had a quick laugh like Kurt's and made a charming chaperone.

When they arrived in Philadelphia, Kurt took his mother home first. It was nearly midnight, and Lynn was going to stay at Sherry's. Kurt swung into the driveway and deposited their luggage at the front door. "Mind if I have a little talk with Lynn, Sherry?" he asked.

"I'm not your mother and you're of age — I hope!" Sherry fitted her key in the lock. "The door'll be open."

"I'll be right in." Lynn was apprehensive.

Kurt took her hand and led her to a clump of pines at the side of the house. It was too dark to see his face. He caught her close; she was off guard and did not resist.

His kisses moved from her eyes and cheeks to her mouth. She knew she should go, but it was such a comfort to stay. Just another minute, she told herself. Vaguely she felt a sense of shame and guilt, but Kurt's arms were strong. She yielded to the temptation and leaned on him, shaken, wishing she could forget Joel and stay in Kurt's arms without thinking. It was so good to be wanted.

He led her to the door, brushed her ear with his lips, and whispered, "Tomorrow afternoon, darling. I'll take you to N'York with me. I'll take care of you, baby doll. You won't disappoint me?"

Lynn swayed in the current; the undertow swept all caution away. She deliberately touched his ear with her lips and whispered, "I'll go with you, Kurt."

In the house, Sherry teased, "*Now* what! What'd *he* want? I s'pose he thinks he can move in now that Joel — "

Lynn started. "He knew?"

103

"Of course. Word gets around. On the way down to surprise you — it was really my idea to find you, but you'd of thought it was all Kurt's when I put the bug in his ear — anyway, on the way down he made the remark — oh, well — "

"All right, Sherry. I can take it!"

"Said if he were Joel, he wouldn't have let you down like that. He said, 'that blond bomber has Joel tongue-tied only he doesn't know it yet.' "

Lynn put a hand to her throat. A dull ache crept in. Well, *who cares?* She gave an exaggerated yawn. "I've had it, Sherry-werry. Don't wake me till next week this time."

In the morning light Lynn faced herself in the mirror. How *could* she have acted that way? She had agreed to go with Kurt *tonight!*

Sherry sauntered in cheerfully. "So ya made it! Mom wants to know if you'd like cereal or eggs. Whatsa matter?"

"Sherry! I don't know what I was thinking of last night. I told Kurt I'd go on a trip to New York — today!"

"You mean — Lynn, you didn't!"

"I was lonely. Honestly, Sherry, when he asked me, I really wanted to go!"

"You said *yes?*"

"Oh, Sherry, what'll I do? I can't date Kurt. Especially a trip to New York!"

"You know what Carla told us."

"That's just it!"

"Well, call him up and explain — or something — "

Lynn opened her mouth wide and looked in the mirror. "I *could* be getting a sore throat!"

Sherry shook with laughter and rolled backward on the bed, letting her head drop over the side. "Lynn, let's face it, we're both under Kurt's spell. I'll confess, I'd have a real inner battle if he ever asked me to go with him. Of course he never will — funny face, short and skinny ole *me!*"

Sherry's folks took Lynn to Stones and Eemah threw her arms around Lynn. "Welcome home, darling!" Her warmth penetrated, and Lynn's burden grew lighter. She was home.

Sherry left and Lynn looked at the phone. "Eemah — "

"Yes, darling. What's troubling you? You can tell me all about it. For why do you frown?"

"Kurt asked me to go on a date."

"So why you aren't happy?" Eemah threw her arms up in the air. "Kurt is a fine boy. He comes by Gil all these two years since we are knowing him. Go out and have some fun. Kurt will treat you like a queen. Sammy is knowing his father in the business. Mr. Chase is a rich man."

Lynn squirmed. How could she face Sherry and the girls if they knew she went on a date with Kurt to New York? A thrill of apprehension made her tingle. But a long empty evening stretched before her and a longer weekend lay ahead. She was so alone, and she wanted to go with Kurt. With him the hours would fly.

"You see, Eemah," she said, "it's like this. I love someone else. I don't want to get too involved — "

"So, you aren't marrying the guy!" Eemah's laugh was light and musical. "Have a good time, Leen. Your other boy friend, whoever he is, would want you should have fun. It isn't right that a young girl like you should be sitting at home. I am telling Gil the same. I said all the girls you are dating are going out with the boys and you are wondering why. He likes one girl should stick by him. I said to him you are crazy already! Go out with the girls. You'll find one when comes the time."

Lynn made herself say, "I guess so. It does seem silly to get too serious over one — especially in high school."

The phone rang. Eemah nodded and Lynn lifted the receiver. She was relieved that Eemah went to the kitchen.

20

KURT'S BARITONE RUMBLE swept her back under; she was unable to resist. "I can't wait to see you, darling. How soon can you be ready?"

"Kurt, I don't want you to rush me. I don't mean about getting ready to go — I mean — "

105

"I know, kid. You can trust me. I lost my head last night; you sweep me off my feet every time I see you. Don't worry, Lynn. I just want to show you around the city. We'll have a time. Couldn't help hearing about that lousy deal you had on Sunday morning at church. I happen to know this Worthington gal — friends of mine who know her — but, well, some other time. Why spoil our big day? Only thing — "

"What, Kurt?"

"I'm not sure you'll enjoy the evening. Y'see, I swing with this jazz band until four in the morning. But we'd have all evening together until eleven bells when I check in at the *Spot*. I phoned my buddy to reserve you a room at the university center. They have guest rooms there. No, you don't! Not one word — you're my guest. Tell you what, Lynn. If you would rather not go with me to this night spot, I'll take you straight to the center and pick you up by ten in the morning. Wowie! That's tomorrow! Anyway, I'll show you a good time, Lynn. We'll go sightseeing, have lunch somewhere, go window shopping in the afternoon, have dinner together — just the two of us. How about that?"

With Eemah's opinion bolstering her courage, Lynn said it sounded great. The minute he hung up, she called Sherry to explain. "I simply couldn't say no, Sherry. He is such a gentleman, even though he clowns around a lot. I really like him."

Sherry was shocked. "You have no business going out with him, Lynn Hale! I'm surprised at you! You know what the Bible says about being unequally yoked together with unbelievers."

"Well, I'm not marrying him, am I?"

"I don't know. That's entirely up to *you*. Good-by!"

Sherry was mad at her. She placed the receiver slowly; the weekend had lost its glamour. Was it easier to forget pain by running away to play, or to bear the pain and wear it out in the daily grind?

Kurt was on his way; she must hurry. It was too late to back out. Besides, what was wrong in going sightseeing with a friend? After all, as Eemah would say, there's no harm in going with a nice guy like Kurt. He isn't mixed up with Hal's cult like Carla was, and maybe I can be of some help to him.

Lynn slammed the train case shut, her hands trembling. Tears of frustration blinded her. *I don't care!* I'm not doing anything wrong. Kurt likes me and wants my company. What's wrong with wanting to be with someone who cares about you?

She walked out to meet him.

The lemon yellow car purred in the drive, and her fears melted. Kurt's father was at the wheel with Mrs. Chase beside him. Kurt leaped from the back door. Lynn kissed Eemah and ran down the steps.

The intimate caress of his glance made her senses reel. But she was safe; they were riding with his parents. She could trust Kurt to respect her wishes. Besides, everyone liked him — even Sherry who disapproved of her dating him.

Mrs. Chase smiled at her. "Kurt's car went to the garage this morning. He was terribly disappointed — wanted you all to himself. Can't say that I blame him."

Mr. Chase explained, "We're due for dinner at the Waldorf. Mother and I phoned in reservations for two more and Kurt agreed this one time, simply because he knows he won't have to pick up the tab. Neither will I, for that matter — it's on the company."

Lynn cried, "Oh, Mrs. Chase! I'm not dressed for a place like that!"

Kurt pulled her arm through his and leaned his head on her shoulder. "You're the sweetest kid. Mom, I told you she wasn't aware of her potential. I predict heads will turn when this golden goddess walks in."

"Yah!" Lynn scoffed. "Heads will turn and women will whisper, 'What's Woolworth doing in Saks Fifth Avenue?'"

Kurt laughed until he had to mop his eyes. The light laughter up front was musical, but Mrs. Chase gave her a searching glance. "You look perfect, my dear. A dark silk like that is always acceptable. Don't worry one minute. We want you to enjoy yourself."

"We'll make time on the New Jersey turnpike," Mr. Chase said. He flicked the radio dial to symphony music.

Kurt talked low in her ear. "I've dreamed about you for so long, Lynn lovely. And now you are here beside me."

She stirred uneasily. "Kurt, I'll be honest with you. I love someone else; I'm sure you know that. It doesn't matter what he did, I still love him. And I'll admit I came with you as — a sort of escape from a bad case of heartbreak. Oh, Kurt, forgive me! You've been so kind — I like you a lot — I do appreciate your — "

"Hush, child! You're cracking with clichés, as Hal says."

"Please, leave Hal out of it. I don't want to get mixed up with his new philosophies."

"It's not a new philosophy. Hal is an avowed Hindu. Now look, Lynn, I went with you to a youth rally and heard a man tell his experience of meeting a higher power. So now it's my turn.

"Hinduism is essentially the same idea. Their followers insist on developing powers that are latent in all of us earth creatures. Their aim in life is to stress the spiritual. They believe man is bound tight by the chains of his own machinery — that is, the material things around him — and they want full release from the confines of a crusted culture. For instance: such apprehensions as you showed just now about not conforming to a social pattern. They believe our minds are fettered with prayer wheels of duty imposed on us from our puritan ancestry.

"What's wrong with dropping out of a false society which — as you said — judges people by which store they choose to buy their gunny sack? What difference does it make? Does it make you a different person if you wear a two hundred dollar dress? Aren't you the same girl in a ten ninety-eight number?"

"Maybe." She couldn't help but smile. "But I'd certainly feel better to be dressed appropriately for the occasion."

"Yipe!" He waved his arms in the air to express futility. "All my efforts down the drain. Lynn, that's exactly what I've been *telling* you. Why be a slave to society? Who cares what you wear? Who really cares? If they judge your worth by the money you pay for a coat, they don't give a — a hang — for you. *You!* The inside individual you are! You're just a coat rack, that's all! We've become robots — "

"Kurt! Are you spoiling her trip with that Hindu harangue you gave me?" Mrs. Chase glanced back, humor crinkling from the corners of her eyes.

"Not at all, Mrs. Chase," Lynn assured her. She lowered her voice, "Kurt, is all this a prelude to your song and dance on a 'trip with LSD'?"

Kurt threw back his head and laughed. "Lynn, you're sharp. Are you ever sharp!" He bent his head close to hers. "You're just the kind who would fit into this groove I'm telling you about. It takes a brilliant mind to experience the revelation we have had of our own personalities — even of the great unknown. If only I could explain it so you'd know."

"You have tried all that stuff?" She hoped he was aware of her disgust. She was on guard. "Know what? Your smart Hindu is trying to lift slaves of society only to fit them into another mold — his groovy world of pill swallowers."

"Man, oh man! Hal should hear this!" Kurt's laughter was infectious.

Lynn was happy. Her mind was at ease concerning the ride together, and she was confident of holding her own in Kurt's debate.

They pulled into a rest stop at the Newark interchange and Lynn followed Mrs. Chase to the women's lounge. She wasn't surprised to hear Kurt's mother remark, "That boy! All wrapped up in Hal's university life. Don't take him too seriously, Lynn. It's merely another fad the young people are going for; it'll wear off. I'm quite sure these boys talk much more than they experiment with new ideas. Our young people today have too much intelligence to get into trouble."

Lynn opened her mouth but decided against saying anything. It might be better to let Carla do the talking.

On their way back to the car Mrs. Chase confided, "I'll tell you a little secret. There was actually nothing wrong with Kurt's car; he could have driven you up here. But he had a phone call from Sherry."

"Sherry?"

"Yes. Sherry called and bawled him out for asking you to go with him. It was too cute. She seemed morbidly concerned for your safety. Kurt was amused — said she scratched like a baby kitten — but he solemnly informed her that she need not worry. He told me later that the idea struck him immediately that your church friends might get the wrong impression and make it rough for you, so he told Sherry that you were riding with us and would be properly chaperoned all the way up and back. I thought it was rather thoughtful of him."

"I'll say!" Lynn felt a load lifted. "I'm glad he said that."

Mr. Chase hummed with the radio all the way to the tunnel. Kurt sang snatches of a song in Lynn's ear. A strange tune — something about lovers in India.

She was glad the increased traffic brought Mrs. Chase's comments and Kurt's attention.

They parked the car in a garage and rode the subway to Broadway. Lynn was fascinated by the swiftly moving scenes. "This is fun," she said aloud.

Kurt bent down, "I want you to come back again and again."

She caught her breath; she tried to speak but no words came. He would think she was impressed by his sales talk and it wasn't that — it was the excitement of seeing Manhattan for the first time.

Kurt rented a car and drove up Riverside Drive to show her Hal's university.

"That's where Gil is too?" She was impressed. "It's colossal!"

"We can meet Hal tomorrow. I want you all to myself tonight," Kurt said.

21

THEY DROVE ALONG THE HUDSON, cars gliding past like long silver fish. Inside their spacious car, city sounds were muted.

Lynn felt the force of Kurt's personality. What was he going to tell her? She kept it light. "Know what?"

"No, you tell me."

She tried to laugh. "Sherry's wild about you."

"Well! How about that! I'm a 'lion among ladies' — a most dreadful thing!"

"We girls all wonder — how can you play in a cheap band when you like classical music?"

Kurt looked pleased. "Good question, my fair lady. First, this Manhattan club I'm in does not play 'cheap' jazz. If it weren't that you'd be up all night — "

"No, thanks."

"I'd be glad to play better music — really fed up with the pattern of things — just like that opera singer said. Funny — "

"Yes?"

"That I followed him like I did. He really got through to me. I liked the guy."

Lynn sparkled. "That's because he told you the truth; he was trying to lead you to Christ."

"But, Lynn, I can't accept such a fantastic story. How do you Christians know for sure that Jesus is alive right now?"

"We know He lives because He brought us into contact with God. His Spirit makes us alive to God. He changes our desires. It's like you said once — 'you Bible clubbers are different from the other kids.'"

Kurt grinned down at her. "Just so you stay different from Pauline! I'm not making fun of you kids, Lynn; I admire

111

you. Especially Joel — he's real. But it's like Gil said: there are better Christians than some who *say* they are."

"Of course."

"You agree with that?"

"Yes, and the Bible agrees with it, Kurt. God knows about the different kinds of people. He says some in the church are hypocrites who don't even belong to Him. Some are carnal — that is, weak and sickly — Christians; they are like children who never develop mentally and bring grief to their parents. But always, there are a few spiritual Christians who live for the Lord and allow God to have His way in their lives."

Kurt drove in silence for some time. Then, "It doesn't make sense, Lynn. Don't get me wrong; I'm really trying to understand. But there's Gil — and his grandparents — the nicest people you could know. Surely *they* don't have to accept Jesus. See what I mean?"

"Kurt, there is a reason for God's allowing the Jewish people to go through those horrible sufferings, and you find all the answers in the Bible. You'd see how it all fits together — like a jigsaw puzzle — if you ever took the time to compare the Old and New Testaments.

"In pastor's study of the Tabernacle he showed God's pattern for man's salvation way back there in the days of Moses, which all pointed to Jesus as the Messiah or the Christ sent from God. The picture pieces were laid out in the Old Scriptures, but the Jews can't understand because they have the wrong pieces to complete the puzzle. Their religious books do not lead them to the truth about Jesus. The Stones never read the Bible; they don't know that Christ means Messiah or that their own prophets gave perfect pictures of Him in their inspired writings.

"Isaiah called Him the Branch and described His sufferings as the perfect Lamb of God slain for our sins. Zechariah prophesied more than five hundred years before Jesus appeared on earth and spoke of 'the man, whose name is the *Branch*,' and described His coming to Israel, first as the lowly servant of God who was sold for the price of a man slave — thirty pieces of silver — and then, in the future, His coming to earth as the King of kings in glory. Daniel wrote even

112

before that; he described the exact time Messiah would be crucified — during the existence of the rebuilt city of Jerusalem and of the second temple. *And,* David described the crucifixion scene in detail when he wrote Psalm twenty-two hundreds of years *before* the prophets.

"When Julie and Joel showed these things to the Stones, they had never once heard it before."

Kurt laughed. "Well! I haven't either. You sure know your Bible, Lynn. You're great! I really admire you for going into this thing all the way — never did look up to a halfway Christian. Y'know — I wouldn't mind coming to your church if I weren't tied up here every weekend. I'm making some hard cash and saving it up; maybe I'll have a band of my own some day — "

"Is it worth it? I mean — is that all you really want out of life?"

He stopped the car and she shivered; her hands were cold. Let him think it was from the cool spring air. She allowed him to put an arm around her. He breathed, "Don't sit so far away. This makes it easier to tell you what I really want."

She tensed, turned her face away, and he changed the subject. "What did Carla tell you girls about her 'trip'?"

She was flustered by his sudden question. Her face burned and she was thankful for the dark. "She told us her experience."

"Just what I thought. Now, Lynn, believe me. I listened to you politely and you can listen to me about something *I'm* acquainted with; this LSD is absolutely harmless. Once in awhile — maybe one out of a hundred — has a bad trip. But my brother tells me he went soaring into the realm of the most heavenly symphonies; the music he heard under this 'mind-manifesting' chemical was for the gods. Said he was in a fairyland of melody.

"One of the artists from Greenwich Village told me he saw patterns and colors he'd never even dreamed of; he painted what he saw in this dream fantasy and sold his work for a fabulous price. So his experience was different from Carla's. You see, honey, you have to hear from the satisfied customers. This college prof who got Hal interested in this has taken the trip many times; he is the pioneer of this new experience — says man is on the verge of discovering himself, who he is, and why he is here."

"Oh, Kurt! How dumb! The Bible answered that centuries ago. Doctors declare that LSD can cause genetic damage and can easily injure a person's mind permanently. We've been reading up on it since Carla — since we heard about it — and the ratio is *not* one in a hundred. No, Kurt, I'm not sold on it, no matter how much fun you've had with it."

"Thousands are trying it, Lynn. We're discovering another world; this professor called it a 'bridge to Paradise' — a paradise such as Persian lore never dreamed. Lynn, you have no idea what you would see and feel and hear and smell and taste — *you've never tried it!*"

She moved away from his arm. "And you've never tried God's offer. Kurt, my teacher, Miss Lindy, said that is just what the old serpent, Satan, told Eve: 'You'll be as gods . . .' You'll know things you never knew before; go ahead and take a bite; try it and see for yourself!"

Lynn found herself crying; she was suddenly tired. "I'm so mixed up. I keep thinking — "

"About that sky pilot?" Kurt breathed in her ear. "Why don't you try to forget him? Like now — when you're out with a guy who knows what love is."

"I'm not sure you do."

22

LYNN WAS RELIEVED when Sherry called her on the phone Sunday night. She said, "Sherry I had a perfectly grand time. Kurt is a gentleman — you needn't ever worry about that — and I don't intend to start dating him."

Sherry was friendly but crisp. "I know what a temptation it was for you after the way Joel did. But, Lynn, none of us can understand how you could go with Kurt *anywhere* after what Carla told us."

On Monday Julie's smug little smile angered Lynn. It said, *Mother was right about you.* Julie, her best friend, showed that she had no intention of trying to understand.

But Carla's attitude cut to the heart. Carla walked beside her to class, her eyes brimming with tears. "Lynn! You of all people! I thought we were not supposed to date unbelievers. Lynn, believe me, I'm praying for you. You don't seem to have any idea of what you're letting yourself in for."

Lynn was too choked to say anything in reply.

At lunch the girls gathered at one table as usual but did not talk directly to her. Pauline searched her with gimlet eyes.

Lynn walked through spring bewildered. The girls had definitely cooled toward her; they disapproved of her having dated Kurt. Of course they had reason. But they didn't give her a chance to explain. Julie, who had always shared everything with her, didn't even care enough to scold her. She acted so self-righteous, practically holding her skirts to one side as Lynn passed by, for fear of contamination.

Lynn stopped attending Bible club and Sunday school. She could no longer bear the cold loneliness.

Weeks passed and the girls kept their distance. Only Carla gave her special smiles to include her in the group. The last day of school Lynn was getting dressed for gym when she overheard: "Joel and that Worthington girl are going steady . . ." ". . . isn't it too bad about Lynn? I mean, she had a bad break. First home, then Joel — " The rest was drowned by blasts from the shower stalls around her.

At three-thirty she ran to catch the first bus since Julie and Sherry always took the second one. Who was calling?

"Lynn! Lynn Hale!"

She turned sharply. Oh, no, Pauline! What did *she* want?

Pauline, loaded with books up to her chin, struggled down the walk from school.

Lynn paused impatiently. She would just have to tell her she was too busy to talk.

One eye pierced through the hair hanging in Pauline's

face. She panted, "Lynn, do me a favor, will you? I have Dad's car around the corner. Help me carry this stuff. There's a storm coming up. This wind's terrible."

Lynn tied a blue scarf over her blowing hair.

Pauline said, "Hey, that's just like mine," as she dropped the stack of books to the sidewalk and tied her own blue scarf.

Lynn picked up half the load and said, "Hurry! I have to catch the bus."

They approached a rusted black car and Lynn prepared to drop her books in the grass. But Pauline cried, "Lynn! I just remembered! I dropped the car keys in my locker. I can't leave these books here — please, Lynn, stay here a sec — I'll hurry. I'll take you home. The sky is getting black."

"Well, hurry up, Pauline." Lynn didn't want to meet any of the girls.

Pauline left at a trot. *The first time I've seen her move out of low gear!* Lynn leaned against the car. The Stones had been so kind to her, but she couldn't impose any longer. She'd have to find a job and rent a room somewhere. Anywhere, just to get away from these *friends* who had betrayed her.

A shriek of tires rounding the corner interrupted her thoughts. Some hot rod tearing the pavement to celebrate school's end. The wind tore at her chiffon scarf and blew a mass of hair across her face. She ducked her head against a spray of rain.

The car ground to a halt ahead of Pauline's. She heard doors open and a scrape of shoes on gravel. Suddenly she glanced up and was panic stricken. Three tough fellows in tight jeans, leather jackets, and unkept hair bent over her. The closest one held a gleaming knife against her side.

"You're comin' with us. See?" The point of the blade pressed through her sweater.

She winced. Two of them gritted their teeth and snarled oaths. "Now git! Paulie the preacher."

It was a mistake. She gasped for breath. "I'm not Paul — " but one on each side grabbed her under the elbows and

116

pushed her to the waiting car. "You're outa your gourd, girlie. We know who ya are."

The fourth one at the wheel hissed through set teeth, "Get her outa sight back there!"

They pushed her down to the floor; she struggled to relieve the painful position. The lean one raised a foot. "Down, dog! Lie down and stay!" She curled up as best she could and leaned her face on her arms. The two in back pushed rudely at her with their big shoes, forcing her to kneel face down for more protection. One kept up a tattoo with his feet. She would be black and blue.

The one with the black beard jabbed her in the neck with his switchblade each time she tried to change positions. Once she screamed, "I'm *not* Pauline. You've made — " and was stopped by a kick on her mouth. She licked blood from her lip.

Lynn groaned inwardly: *save* me. She could not pray; she felt dead inside.

Their oaths were coarse; she had never heard such filthy remarks. She tried to close her mind to the words, but she gathered bits of information in the course of an hour. They were heading for New York City.

After another hour on the highway her back and legs ached painfully. She groaned, "I've got to sit up." She tried to stretch; severe cramps brought moans to her throat. She turned her face toward the bearded one.

He pulled her to the seat beside him. "Say! She's not ugly at all. Whadda know! Stop at the tavern in Jersey, Russ, and let's show her a good time."

She struggled in protest; the lean one pulled her to his side. "She's in for a treat. Bet she's never had a boy friend. Too busy preachin — "

The driver snapped, "We'll keep moving, you fools. Craig wants to show her the good time. See? Light up. That'll keep her in a good mood. Don't want no trouble."

"Yeah, man." The beard bristled on her neck.

Lynn's throat ached. She tried to cry out. "I'm *not* — " but was terrified as they stopped her with pressure from big, dirty hands. She felt herself trembling violently. Her shaking was soon noticed. The lean one soothed, "Don't rattle your bones like that! We're out ta show ya whatcha been missin. In a few minutes you'll be calm and quiet like a purring kitty cat. Watch."

She was frozen with fear. The two fellows produced tiny, short-stemmed pipes. The beard took an envelope from his pocket and stuffed both pipes. The lean one gave Lynn a smirk which showed crooked, yellow teeth. "I'll roll the little lady some green grass." He poked a small white paper into a cigarette, then paused to light his pipe.

A strange odor permeated the car. Lynn felt tears running down her face. Her body trembled; she was nauseated from fright.

"You'll get so ya love it." The lean one's mottled face came close to hers. His breath made her sick. "Here. Put this in your mouth, Paul-*een*. The real stuff — Brooklyn green. When you're up tight it loosens yer nerves. One guy lit up last week and he quoted a long Psalm. Oughta bring out the preacher in ya."

She jerked away. The beard's hand pressed into her side; she cried out in pain. He said softly, "We mean business, sis. Ya don't say no to us. And prayin' won't help this time. This ain't no church. I said *take* it! *Smoke!*"

She felt the cigarette between her teeth. The lean one swore. "Drag!"

She drew in. *"Prayin' won't help this time."* She sent up a silent call. *Lord, I can't help myself. Please —*

Pauline would get back to the car; she would think Lynn had left her; she would be mad but not alarmed. Eemah would just think she was busy with last-minute school activities. No one knew where she was!

Smoke saturated the car. The fellows leaned back, thrust their feet out, sang, and laughed. Gradually they grew less rowdy. It wasn't too bad if she leaned back and relaxed; she would quit struggling.

The pressure lifted; she felt slightly giddy. Her head sagged to one side; the beard leaned her on his shoulder and sang languidly. "You're comin' high, girl . . . we'll bring you back down, girl . . . you're all right, baby. Any girl's all right with me." He laughed until he doubled up with mirth.

Russ began to sing and tap his foot on the gas pedal in rhythm. Pete complained, "Cut it out!" Russ's voice sounded thick when he answered.

Lynn let her head drop over; she needed a long time to think.

23

LYNN JERKED AND HIT HER HEAD on the front seat. I'm trapped! Let me out!"

Pete flung out his hand and shoved her back. She cried weakly and leaned against the bearded one. It would be better to stop fighting. The buzzing steadied; the sweet aroma made her thirsty. If only she had a drink of pure, sparkling water.

The beard said softly, "Let's go ta the Boheme dance 'stead of — "

Russ barked, "We're taking her *there* first."

Pete grumbled, "Barr better pay off tonight. I'm broke."

Lynn relaxed and fell into a doze. A sudden draft of fresh air revived her. The car windows were open in front. The sky was black and rain spattered the windshield. They were in Manhattan.

These fellows must be Craig's pals. They were all in the same groove — Kurt and Hal, in the upper bracket of intellectuals with their symphonic sound, and these crude hairy apes were all deluded by the same devil.

In a sudden illumination, Bible verses memorized at the retreat crossed her mind. She murmured, " . . . the god of this world has blinded the unbelievers' minds . . . preventing them from seeing the illuminating light of the Gospel of the glory of Christ, the Messiah, Who is the image and likeness of God."

The lean one slapped his knee and chortled, "She's preachin'! She's preachin'!"

Pete flung back, "Keep it up, Pauly. Atta girl, Paul-een."

Quoting the verses helped ease a burden somehow. She closed her eyes against the flashing lights along the thruway. The verses kept coming to mind. *Lo, I am with you always, even unto the end of the world . . .*

It seemed like night when they finally pulled up in an alley behind ancient brownstone houses. She followed them meekly, the knife gleaming at her side. It was Craig's plot; he was getting even with Pauline for her jibes the past year. *When he discovers it's me, what will he do?*

They climbed a dark stairway two flights. A door opened and a girl rushed into Pete's arms.

They pushed her into the room and Lynn smelled a sudden rush of sweet air. A group was sitting in a circle on the bare floor staring at burning candles. The air was thick. She gagged and clutched her throat.

A girl grabbed her by the arm, dragged her to a small bedroom, and heaved her onto a lumpy cot. She left, closing the door behind her.

After her eyes penetrated the shadows, Lynn saw a form on a bed across from her. She started. Carefully raising herself on one elbow, she looked, her arm trembling violently. A streak of lightning seared the dark; in the eerie light she saw a girl's upturned face. The eyes were staring at the ceiling.

Thunder shook the window frame, but the girl did not move. Lynn's heart raced. It was Jodi!

In the music room the Bible club came to a close. Julie, standing in front, said, "That's it, girls. Thanks for remaining faithful to the end. The boys couldn't wait for the bell to clear out their lockers and leave for the summer."

Sherry bounced up excitedly. "Didn't you say Joel and Gil were on their way home? When'll we see them?"

Julie sat down at one of the desks and put her head in her hands.

Carla, tying on a rain hat, stepped across the aisle to pat her head. "Cheer up, Julie; vacation is here at last. All we have to do now is go job hunting. But weren't you leaving for Nyack to attend music school for the summer term?"

"What's the matter, Julie pal?" Sherry bent over to see her face.

Julie's eyes were wet. They all stopped talking and took seats around her. "Girls, I can't get over Lynn. I'm sorry to dampen your spirit today, but she is never completely out of my mind.

"I scolded Joel for what he did Easter Sunday; then Mother reprimanded me for scolding him. They — we all — were so sure he had met the ideal girl; they were practically engaged from the start."

Sherry pouted. "I still think he made a mistake, letting Lynn down with no explanation. That Natalie seems awfully snooty, I think. Whoops — me and my big mouth! Skip it, Julie."

"It's all right." Julie kept looking down at the desk. "I do happen to know — "

"What?"

"Well — Natalie is — but it's all over now. It's too late to look back. What I'm saying is, we must not give up hope for Lynn. Lynn's behavior could keep her from fellowship with the Lord and with us — for years to come."

Carla paced the floor. "This is a fine thing! Who's so self-satisfied around here? Are *we* completely blameless? Not one of us made a real effort to bring her back. Not one of us has been a real friend when she needed us most." She broke into weeping. "She cared about me — came out in the hall after me that day — "

Sherry also broke down. Julie wondered at herself. Was this cool attitude she felt *self-righteousness?* For the first time she faced it. Yes, she *had* passed by on the other side. She was the religious Pharisee. And she *knew* Lynn was suffering from their censure.

They were surprised to see her cry. "Carla, you are right. I *have* felt superior to Lynn. But I had no right to. She's been a better Christian than I — always so conscious of God's will for her life. I'm going to start praying — in faith believing this time — that God will bring her back quickly."

They gathered their stacks of books and descended to the main hall.

Someone bounded through the double doors and took the steps two at a time.

Craig bumped into them, staring wildly from one to the other. "Any of you seen Lynn?"

His shouts alarmed them. Julie felt the thrill of fear. It was the second time this afternoon that Lynn was strangely impressed upon her heart. "Why?" she cried.

"I just saw *Pauline*. At her *car*. She was mad. But Lynn wasn't there — "

They saw his face pale; sweat drops glistened on his face. "You haven't seen her? Are you *sure?*"

Carla scowled. "What are you so worried about?"

Craig pounded his fists together. "I've gotta dig out for N'York — on the double!" He sped down the stairs and out of sight.

Sherry gasped, "Let's find Pauline and ask her."

They were halfway down the block when a car pulled to the curb. Gil waved from the open window; Joel was driving.

Julie cried, "Are we ever glad to see you! And I wasn't expecting you until late tonight, Joel."

Gil jumped out and let her in the front seat. He held the back door for Sherry and Carla, then climbed in beside Julie.

Joel said, "Good to see you again. Sure have missed that Friday club. Gil and I took off from Morningside Heights early but he had an errand or two."

Gil laughed, "He is so good to me. Waited a half hour or more in the library while I did a little research. How are you, Julie darling?"

The girls talked at once; they wanted to question Pauline about Craig's strange words.

Joel drove to Porter's house.

Pauline shuffled out in floppy slippers and stared at the girls on the step.

Julie said, "Pauline, do you know why Craig was so excited? He mentioned something to us about you and Lynn. Then he ran away and we couldn't find out — "

Pauline shook the hair from her face and exclaimed loudly in her whine, "Yes, I know! And *it serves her right* for running around with those hoodlums — Craig and Kurt both! The Lord showed who was in the right when He let 'em take *her* for a ride instead of *me!*"

"A ride!" Carla's cry was a hoarse whisper.

Julie clasped Pauline's arms. She fairly shouted, "Tell us what happened!"

Gil and Joel, sensing trouble, came running, Sherry following.

Pauline tossed her head; her eyes gleamed with pleasure at the opportunity of telling her story. She ended in triumph, "So when I told Craig I'd left her at the car until I found my keys, he got all excited and said under his breath 'why didn't those dumb acid heads see the difference in you — her with red hair.' And I told him we both had head scarves on and he shouted how he hated me and wished I'd drop dead. He'd planned a little surprise party for me in New York — and I saw through the whole thing! I laughed right in his face and I told him, 'Your little scheme boomeranged, didn't it, Craig Barr? That's because *I* am above reproach and God is punishing *her* for running around with you nut heads.' I'm sure not going to shed a tear — she got *just what she deserved!*"

Joel looked at her with scorn. "Pauline, if each of us got what we deserved, we would never be saved in the first place, let alone be called by the name *Christian*." He wheeled and bounded down the steps.

24

As THEY DROVE OFF Joel said, "I think we'd better contact Kurt. He might be able to help us."

Julie nodded. The girls in back were quiet. Gil put his arm across Julie's shoulders. "We could phone from a booth at this gas station."

"Good idea." Joel pulled off the street. "I'll take care of it. Meanwhile you all keep praying. I don't like the sound of this."

Julie couldn't keep back the tears. "Oh, Gil! She is the sweetest girl in the world. I can't bear to think — "

Gil put his face next to hers. "You are the sweetest girl I've ever met." Then he turned his head to remark, "You two might as well know. I've asked Julie to be my wife."

Sherry shouted, "That means one thing!"

"Yes," Julie told them, "he decided for Christ. Only he has had a terrific conflict for several weeks — about telling his grandparents."

Gil's voice was low. "My father won't be too disturbed although he won't like it. But my grandmother and grandfather — it will break their hearts! I simply cannot tell them yet. They mean *everything* to me!"

"Everything?" Carla echoed in a whisper. "Didn't *He* suffer for our sakes, Gil?"

"I see what you mean." Gil bowed his head for a minute. "I know I must tell them but it won't be easy."

Joel stayed in the booth a long time. They were tense when he got in.

"Kurt was home. When I told him all we'd heard, he went into high gear. I've never heard him like that. Said he'd called Stones twice, but Gil's grandmother said each time that Lynn had not come home from school. So he was beginning to wonder when I called.

"Now I don't know whether or not I did the right thing; he's mad enough to kill Craig. He's tearing out in that little foreign job right this minute – and will probably overtake Craig in that jalopy of his. What should we do?"

Carla said soberly, "God is able to protect Lynn. But I'd feel better if we could *do* something to help."

"So would I!" Sherry brushed her sleeve across her eyes. "She's with guys who are out of their heads half the time."

"All the time," Carla corrected. "Their minds are controlled by the devil; they really believe those drugs – with their meditations – are going to show them the secrets of the universe. There they are – I can see them yet – groping about in some smoke-filled room completely out of their heads."

Joel sat at the wheel, staring at the phone booth. "Earthly, sensual and devilish, God says. And Lynn is their captive! Let's pray right now for her protection. God is able."

Lynn sat up shakily. It was too dark to see. Was that a small lamp on the dresser? Clinging to the cot and the wall, she crossed the space. She turned on the light and stood still, watching the door.

No one came. She moved quietly to the bed. "Jodi?" she whispered.

The dark eyes rolled slowly from their upward position and tried to focus. The pupils were pinpoints of black in brown pools. She stared vacantly.

"You are sick, Jodi." Lynn touched the girl's cold forehead. She pulled up a cover and jerked back as Jodi's arm shot out. The white inner arm was streaked with gashes. Evidence of the needle was unmistakable.

The door opened. Lynn staggered back. It was an older girl who looked as though she had seen multitudes of morbid cases like this. Her expression was bored indifference as she sat down. "I have to baby-sit you two until a medic comes for this chick and a guy named Barr comes for you."

"Is she – " Lynn whispered, sinking to the edge of the cot.

"Might as well be. She's taken an overdose again. Mac'll

125

bring her around. Don't let it bug you. I'm on my last term here and I've seen everything."

Lynn choked with bitterness, "Some education! What good does it do?"

"I've wondered the same thing."

The girl's hair was yellowish white, stiff as straw from bleaching. Her face, caked with layers of makeup, looked old, but she could be in her early twenties. *She's done everything and is utterly dissatisfied!*

Lynn felt weakness numb her body. She lay back and closed her eyes. How could God love this sick world of rebels? *God so loved . . . that he gave.* Was it too late to save Jodi?

The girl was talking in a hollow monotone. "I came to New York from a town in Ohio: Tried to make friends. No luck. Too straight. Had to start swingin' to *belong.* Now I can't go home; my folks'd die if they knew I was hooked.

"That's her trouble — she's hooked. Her dad gives her an allowance in four figures, so she buys all the *green* she wants. An uptown smoothie named Chase sold her a ticket to paradise — but for her it turned out to be hell.

"Oh, not at first. She had good trips at first. Then a hard one — guess it was a bad trip from the word 'go.' Went straight down to the cellular consciousness where she saw herself as a mass of bloody tissue. She was sure she was dead. Had nightmares for weeks after. I've never had one like that yet!

"Then this cat Chase gave her the bounce — refused to have any more to do with her. Guess she was really hooked on him, too. I met her on this millionaire playboy's yacht. Friend of mine got me a date with him two years ago. I would have jumped in the river if he hadn't introduced me to these."

Lynn shuddered. The girl produced a tiny glassy-looking envelope. She waved it in Lynn's face, then stuck it in her pocket. "Don't ever touch it. Better jump in the river."

"Heroin?" Lynn's voice was hoarse.

The girl nodded and gestured toward Jodi. "He fixed her

up too. She was up tight and would have cracked up if she didn't get some rest."

Lynn cried, "But it's a false rest! It's the devil's rest. Only Christ can give you the real quietness of heart you need."

The girl's hollow laugh was shaky. "They said you'd start preaching."

Lynn walked unsteadily to the girl and touched her arm. "Please help me get away. They thought I was — but that doesn't matter now. Will you — "

The door opened and a young man strode to the bed. He picked up Jodi's wrist and looked at his watch.

Lynn was surprised. He was handsome and well-groomed, with a professional manner — probably a young intern from the university hospital.

He turned abruptly and left the room. The girl said, "He looked worried."

"Please! I've got to get out of here before — "

"Listen!" The girl stood by the window looking out at the rain. "I like you. You're square but I like you. Don't ever change; stay away from — "

Lynn was desperate. "Please! Think! What can I do?"

"Cool it!" The girl leaned against the dresser. "Those cats that brought you here aren't around now. When the pot party is going strong, I'll sneak you out."

Lynn sank to the cot, weak from relief. The house was strangely quiet. Two fellows came in and carried Jodi away. Lynn fought panic. Was she in a bad dream? Could all this be real?

The girl said tonelessly, "I'll have a look around." She was gone several minutes. "Luck." She motioned Lynn to follow.

Lynn held back. "Will it make trouble for you? What will they do to you?"

"What more can they do to me? C'mon!"

Lynn followed her downstairs. At the door a man in a plaid sports coat and black cap took Lynn's arm. Lynn looked sharply at the girl.

Her green eyes narrowed. "Follow Bernie. He'll take you where you want to go."

"Who *are* you?" Lynn searched the stranger's face. He was an older man. Hard lines creased his cheeks and his mouth hardly opened when he spoke.

"You want to get out of here — so whatcha stallin' for? Get movin'. I'm not waitin' see?" He kept one hand in his pocket and the other on her elbow.

They walked down the street to a parking lot. He opened a car door and she staggered in. *Lord, save me. I am your child.* The anguished prayer brought a flicker of life to her soul.

"Get your head down on the seat and keep it down!"

They drove for an eternity of minutes. She knew they were on city streets by the traffic roar. In the lull of a stop light she asked, "Why didn't she keep me there?"

He sounded pleased. "She's smart, that's why. She hasta make cash in fist every day of her life, that's why."

Lynn waited for him to go on. "I don't see — "

He burst into uproarious laughter. "That was purty slick; she's the smart one. That young duck comes after you and she gives 'im a good line. 'Someone spirited the little preacher outa here, but I have contacts. Pay me some greenbacks and I'll see wot I kin do ta find her for ya.'" His laughter was swallowed in the roar of moving metal.

Lynn trembled. His words indicated that someone would be searching for her. It would be Craig of course.

"Sit up!"

She jerked up and looked out at what appeared to be an estate.

"Keep your mouth shut and let me do the talkin'." The man drew up to a side entrance and unlocked the door. They went along a dim corridor to an elevator. He pushed a button and they descended to a lower level.

They entered a large room outfitted as a dispensary. A girl dressed in nurse's uniform came through another door.

Bernie jerked his chin toward Lynn and mumbled, "Needs a little — enough to keep her comfortable till her boyfriend shows. Here's her tag." He handed the nurse a paper.

Lynn's heart pounded until her cheeks flamed scarlet.

128

Her mind raced. There must be some way of escape. As she bolted, the man grabbed her arms.

The nurse looked at her face. "You're high, all right! It hits some like that. We'll see what we can do for you." She selected a hypodermic needle from instruments in a drawer.

Lynn sagged and the man dragged her to a chair. The nurse injected the needle; a streak of fire entered Lynn's arm.

Then the man winked at the nurse and left.

25

LYNN PRESSED A HAND to her throat. "Do you have a rest room?"

The girl acted like it was routine. "Right down the hall to your left. But hurry back; you look ill." She opened a door and Lynn walked unsteadily through.

A glance back showed the girl watching. Lynn found the rest room and splashed cold water on her face. Voices reached her. She opened the door a crack and saw two fellows with the nurse. One acted delirious; the other was trying to hold him upright. *They have her attention!*

Lynn slipped around the corner to a stairway. Thick carpeting carried her soundlessly upstairs. She ran down a hall, muffled sounds from below adding to her fear. She must hide! They were following her.

She stopped by a door in the shadows, quietly turned the knob, and stepped through. She edged along the wall to a heavily curtained doorway and parted the curtain carefully at eye level.

Several fellows and girls seemed in a state of stupor. A girl walked dazedly across the floor, her eyes closed, hands outstretched, groping for something in a dark world of fantasy. A boy, lying on the floor with hands over his eyes, laughed — a high, uncanny laugh that shot needles through her veins.

Lynn crept into the room, eased along the dark wall, and gazed at the shadowy figures in horror. Another boy sat staring at a flowered pattern on a footstool, saliva dripping from his open mouth. He looked crazed, sitting there staring and drooling over a flower like a retarded child.

A flowered curtain moved and a tall man glanced around. It was Hal Chase!

Lynn flattened herself against the shadowy wall. When he disappeared, she sank to her knees in a darkened corner and tried to become part of the scene.

Joel said, "Somehow I haven't any peace. We should do something!"

Carla rubbed her arm across her eyes. "I'm with you. I'll not rest tonight until we find out — "

"Carla! Would you know how to locate places Craig's gang might hang out?"

Gil sat forward. "I was just thinking the same thing, Joel. I suggest we call home and tell our folks we're off on a jaunt to celebrate the end of school. Then we'll take the freeway. You said that Craig has a slow car?"

"I'll phone first!" Sherry scrambled out and ran to the phone booth.

On the way out of town Carla commented, "Kurt isn't one bit closer to accepting Christ. And he said to me this week, 'You sure have changed, Carl.' So I told him the old life was gone, buried, and I was glad of it and didn't even miss it! I said Christians had prayed for me and Christ had rescued me from the 'power of darkness.' He just gave me a sour grin and walked away."

Gil said, "And you Christians prayed for *me*. Now the Bible makes sense to me."

Gil drew Julie close within his arm. "And I'm glad you and Joel cared enough to study my religious viewpoint so you could talk to me about God. If only I can show my precious grandparents that this same Jesus is their coming King. But when I first tell them, I know it will break their hearts. They will sing the Shemah and call me a 'traitor to our race' like I did that opera singer. Do you know what got through to me that night? When Mills said 'you are dead to God,' I knew he was right.

"And you kids were so sure of your faith. You didn't start a club because your church ordered it. It wasn't a tradition with you or a duty to be performed to merit entrance to heaven. You did it because you actually *know* God and wanted others to know Him."

Gil continued, "I compared my friends with the Evans's. As good as my people are, they are afraid of death; they have no hope.

"Their conversation rotates on one theme: I — me — mine. What I possess and what I want to possess. Any family to-day without a fat bank account, a swimming pool, lake resort cottages, and yachts isn't worth knowing.

"Julie, your folks have a lovely home, but I could see that their conversation centered on spiritual things. You were all conscious of God and His desires — not your own. It was this difference in basic attitudes that began to change my mind. I willingly turned from a dead religion to a living Lord."

They drove on, each absorbed in his own thoughts. Finally Joel remarked, "I read the other day that there were fifteen thousand arrests last year for marijuana users."

Gil nodded. "And I heard up at school that pressure is being exerted to legalize all these drugs. It's the same premise Hal had in his talk about 'usage makes correct.' If enough people use something, this is supposed to prove that we should make it legal.

"I asked a guy on campus what he was thinking about when he smoked pot. He said, 'Thinking? Why, nothing at all. Nothing but getting *into* it — just getting into it as far as I can go.' "

Joel said, "Yep, they're all looking for escape from the realities of life. Anything to blot out their minds — as Carla told us."

Carla leaned over Julie's shoulder. "I can't understand

131

what's happened to Jodi. She's missed the last two weeks of school."

Sherry sniffed. "She prob'ly blotted out her mind like the others and forgot to come back."

Julie sighed. "Her main argument against us was the one her father harangued on. 'Any belief in God and the Bible is an emotional crutch; you don't need religion or God; you are the master of your own fate and the captain of your own soul.'"

Gil shrugged. "So they go all out for 'mind-busting drugs,' but of course *that* isn't an emotional crutch. Wow! How inconsistent can you get? But they're traveling on a dead end road."

"What's going on up ahead?" Joel asked.

The rain spattered, limiting visibility. Gil opened his window and leaned out. Traffic jam ahead. Better slow down, Joel."

Soon they were creeping in a line of cars. Flashing lights from police cars pierced the blackness ahead.

"Must be quite a wreck," Julie said.

They opened their windows and looked around as the car slowly moved forward, inching toward the police cars. An officer waved traffic to the median strip with his flashlight. They passed close to a semitrailer jackknifed on a curve. The body of the truck had landed across the highway, blocking northbound traffic for miles.

They heard the distant wail of a siren. Sherry cried, "It's Kurt! That's his car!"

"Where?"

Joel braked although the officer was waving him on. They looked sharply to their right and saw a small foreign car twisted beside the cab of the truck. At the same instant they saw the other car in the ditch.

"It's Craig's old jalopy!" Carla screamed out, as Gil shouted, "It *is!* Stop, Joel!"

"Keep moving!" the officer shouted.

Joel advanced with traffic on the median until they found a wider place to pull out of line and stop. He snatched his keys. "You girls stay here! Gil and I —"

They were gone. Sherry wailed, "Let's go with them, Julie!"

"Better not," Julie advised.

Carla moaned, her knuckles rubbing her mouth.

Julie held up her wrist to look at her watch. "It's only six-thirty and look how dark the sky is."

"They skidded on the curve!" Sherry's words chattered from her shaking.

"Pray for them!" Carla cried. "They are not ready to die! Oh, Kurt! I'm going over there, Julie!" She bounded from the car.

The others followed. They stepped through soggy grass and made their way back down the road to the wreck. Cars paused to let them through. The officer shouted, "Stay in your cars! Keep moving!"

Julie heard Carla's cry, "We know them!" and his reply, "Keep out of the way, lady!"

The girls melted into the shadows along the truck body and inched their way around the wreck to the other side. They caught sight of the boys by the jalopy. Two men were leaning over the car. As they approached, they saw the car lying on its side in the ditch, the front end smashed.

Sherry gasped aloud and Julie warned, "Keep quiet."

Carla, who had been so eager to get there, stopped short and clung to Sherry.

Julie whispered, "I'll see if Joel can tell us anything." She caught a glimpse of Craig in the front seat and turned her face away. Horror gripped her. She gazed fascinated, as the man in a black coat and white clergy collar intoned in a low tone, "Don't worry, son. Everything's going to be all right."

Joel and Gil stood behind the man, waiting. Joel seemed agitated. Julie crept closer.

The siren sounded nearer; the ambulance must have come from some distance.

From a gurgling voice, Julie heard the word *die.* Then she heard Craig distinctly say *Joel.*

Joel called, "I'm *here,* Craig." The clergyman stepped aside and Joel looked down through the broken window.

133

Julie heard Carla's muted cry, "Dear God, save him now!"

Then Joel staggered back. Gil helped him away, motioning Julie to follow. "Don't look in!"

Julie kept close to the girls; they waited for Joel to recover. He whispered, "Where's Kurt?" and stumbled over the uneven ground. They walked around the cab of the trailer and came upon a group by the roadside. Two bodies were stretched out on the ground, both covered with blankets. An officer stood by.

"Kurt?" Joel called gently.

They heard a groan; and one of the forms moved. Joel fell on his knees beside him.

Julie edged closer. Gil put his arm around her and she cried against his coat. He motioned to the girls, and they stumbled back to the parked car.

No one spoke. The night wind carried the siren ever closer. Finally, after an eternity of waiting, the ambulance screamed down upon them, crossed the median, and pulled up beside the wreck.

26

LIGHTNING FLASHED THROUGH THE SKY; the thunder rolls tumbled into one another, subsiding to a low mumble in the distance.

Gil kept his arm around Julie. "Good thing we followed Joel's hunch and came up here."

The ambulance tore out, scattering traffic right and left.

Finally Joel returned. He said, "Police questioned me a long time about Kurt — they say he caused the accident. Tire marks — he evidently scooped in ahead of Craig and made him brake hard, which made the truck turn to get around them. It jackknifed, pulling Kurt's little car like a

134

toy. Craig's was folded like an accordion between." He leaned his head over the wheel.

Julie stroked the back of his head. The silence uncovered Sherry's low sobs. Joel shuddered. "Dear God!" He took a handkerchief and mopped his face.

An officer approached. "Better sit still a few minutes, Evans. Get hold of yourself before you drive."

Joel nodded. Gil said, "Thank you, sir."

Then Joel told them. "Did you hear what Craig said to that preacher — so called — Gil?"

"No, I didn't."

Julie said, "Didn't Craig call for you, Joel? How did he know — "

"He didn't know I was there, yet he called my name. The backward collar kept up a croon about nothing. When I first got there, he was trying to give Craig some kind of false comfort in dying.

"Craig was all — he was dying. Engine smashed through to him." Joel bent double, his face contorted. "And that man calls himself a *minister!* I've *got* to be one. Julie, I've *got* to! That man is a criminal. He deliberately withholds the saving grace of God and lets dying men think they are perfectly safe going out to meet God *alone!*

"Craig was gasping for breath. His face was so bloody I couldn't bear to look. But his mind was working! He literally gasped for each breath and he said, '*Not* all right — going to die!' Then he said my name and I looked in. His throat was filling; he had only a few minutes left. I thought he said it was too late, and I told him about the thief on the cross who acknowledged Jesus as Lord and asked for salvation. I said, 'Craig, He suffered and died for *you.* God will forgive your sins. Trust Him now.'

"His eyes cleared for just a second, as though he *knew.* Then — "

They all shuddered. Carla whispered. "And Kurt?"

Joel came back with a start. "Oh! Yes! I'll tell you. Craig's condition was so awful that I've forgotten everything else. I trust he made that final contact with God. If

135

he did — we know 'the blood of Jesus Christ cleanses from *all* sin.' " Joel took a deep breath of the cool air.

"Kurt was thrown clear of his little car — a miracle, they said. He and the truck driver have injuries, but they were both conscious.

"Listen! Kurt seemed to be almost delirious with fear for Lynn. He literally begged me to go straight to lower Manhattan — made me write down two addresses. And he gave me Jodi's phone number — some house east of the campus.

"I hope you can all go with me because I'm going after Lynn!"

Gil said, "Wait! Let me give the police our phone numbers. Tell them just enough about this so they can contact our families back home and tell them what we have to do. Otherwise — "

"Go ahead." Joel seemed relieved. "Girls, go with him and give your phone numbers. And Julie, give the police these addresses Kurt gave me. Honestly, sis, my legs are like water."

Gil drove the car to the tunnel. At a service station Joel took the wheel; and at seven-thirty they pulled up at a burger drive-in. "You give the order while I call Jodi's number," Joel instructed.

He stayed a long time. When he returned Julie said, "Your hamburger is cold!"

He looked at them absently. "A maid at her number gave me three other numbers to call. She said Jodi had not been in her apartment for at least a week.

"A girl answered the next call and tried to cross-examine me, so I said, 'Just tell me where I can reach her. It's important that I contact her.' Didn't tell our names or business — and she gave me these two other numbers to call.

"They were men. The first one sounded slightly British and I didn't get anything out of him. The next voice sounded exactly like Hal!"

Carla squealed, "I'll bet it was! He helps a professor run that big place up the Hudson — the mansion I was telling you about where I took that 'trip.' "

"Well, he flatly refused to tell me anything about her, and I think he suspected who I was. So here we are. On a dead-end street."

Gil shrugged. "How about those two addresses? Can't we follow them?"

Carla agreed. "We can try. Let me go up to the door and ask for Jodi."

Joel took two bites from his sandwich and started the motor. They inquired at filling stations and finally found the first address in a section of brownstone houses. Joel parked the car down the street from the correct address, and Sherry insisted on going with Carla.

They rang the bell. A gray-haired woman of immense proportions filled the screened doorway. She held the inner door with one hand and tried to peer through the screen at the shadowy figures outside. A dim light fixture hung from the wall behind her.

Carla said quickly. "Jodi wanted me to find something she left in a room upstairs."

The woman slammed the door in their faces.

Lynn felt herself fainting. She was hungry! And so sick. *Am I dreaming this nightmare?* The girl kept sleepwalking, hands outstretched, groping like a blind person. A boy daubed paint up and down his arm, a glazed, idiotic smile on his face.

Lynn covered her face with her hands and tried to remember what came before this night. She couldn't bear to look at the scene. These acid heads were living it up, all right, and they would go on living with disoriented minds until they died. Just wait till she saw Kurt. *He'd better not ever mention Hal's nut house religion to me again — ever — as long as I live! If I ever get out of here.*

She had better tie something over her hair; Hal might recognize her. A girl had discarded her clothing and it lay in a pile by the couch. Lynn crawled inch by inch across the dimly lighted space.

Finally she felt safe. With head covered, she crouched down and leaned against a huge chair where she could observe without being noticed. The eerie scene mesmerised her; her head sank lower; her eyes closed and she slept soundly.

Thunder boomed and rumbled into her dream and Lynn awoke with a jerk. Those around her were deep in their various 'trips.' The nausea returned; she wept violently. The months of frustrating mental debate swirled in her mind.

Hal's voice sounded in her consciousness. "If Jodi is dead, it's her own fault. I warned her not to go for the hard stuff."

Lynn stared. Hal stood inside the flowered curtain facing a young man in a beige trench coat. The man's accent sounded British, but his words were too low for her to catch all. "Could ruin you . . . ."

Hal did not lose his suavity. "You won't, Bobby. You know what my testimony against you would do. It would take several of your dad's millions to pull you out of *that* one. You're the guy that started her on the needle. Now *get out!* I don't want any part of it." He sent one of his lightning glances around the room and caught her off guard; she couldn't draw back in time.

He sucked in his breath in a choking sound. As he started for her, Lynn scrambled to her feet and screamed, "I'm sick of it. Do you *hear?* Sick of it! Your paradise — it's — *hell!* Just look at these kids!"

With one long arm he wheeled her past the curtain and into the hall. "How did *you* get in here!" His face was white with fury. Men's voices sounded in the hall, and he jerked his head up to listen.

Bobby bolted for the stairway at the rear. Hal paused, still clutching her. They heard someone's authoritative voice. ". . . warrant . . . crackdown . . . federal narcotics . . ." reached them. Hal's face changed as the men surrounded him.

Lynn, leaning against the wall beside him, still hysterical, felt a white light blind her eyes. Hal's high-pitched wail pierced through, "Don't you dare get that film developed! I'll sue — "

"Oh, no you won't, Mister. You're going to show us around. What have we here?"

They brushed past and entered the room as an officer

propelled Hal by one arm. Lynn flattened herself against the dark wall and slowly retreated. She found the same stairway she had come up.

On the last flight to the basement, she found Bobby poised as though listening. He held up a hand to caution her. Instinctively she slipped noiselessly to the step above him and waited, her head close to his. They were both fugitives and he seemed to know what he was doing.

He was watching the same narrow hall she had traveled earlier. His whispered, "Want to get out, don't you?"

She put a hand on his shoulder to steady herself; she was fearful of fainting. "I've got to find my way back to Philadelphia, but I lost my purse and —"

"There! The nurse is gone," he hissed through closed teeth. "I don't want to be held here for questioning. C'mon!" He grabbed her by the hand and ran down the hall to the dispensary and through a narrow passageway lined with white steel cabinets. There's a back door," he said.

He led her outside through gardens at the rear of the estate to a high hedge. They ran along the hedge for some distance. In a tangle of thorny bushes he parted some branches and she slid through, tearing her hose. They were on a back street.

"We're in luck," he breathed. "You climb in the back and I'll take you straight to Philly. Too hot in this town for me. And say — relieve me of some of this dough —" He tossed a plastic envelope over his shoulder into her lap.

The car glided from the curb. He kept talking, "Money cost me my health and might cost me my life. Do me a favor and use it for something like food. Looks to me like you need it."

She was too tired to reply. She was on the road back — *home!* She knew he was speeding down the highway at a terrific rate, but every mile took her closer to safety. When he pulled into a filling station at an interchange, she opened the door, stepped outside, and fell to the pavement.

27

"Now WHAT?" Carla's mouth trembled.

They climbed back into the car.

Sherry shook from chill and fright. "You'd think she saw a ghost!"

They both explained the woman's strange behavior. Joel made a sharp U-turn to take them in the opposite direction.

"We'll find Broadway and stay with it. I'm going to locate this big place I've heard so much about." Joel wheeled into traffic.

Julie began to shake. "I'm afraid we'll get ourselves in a jam."

Gil leaned his head against hers. "The Lord is my Shepherd . . . I will fear no evil."

"Good for you!" Sherry found her voice. "Why is it that *new* Christians are the ones who show the most faith at times like this? I'll confess I've been slipping."

They had difficulty locating the address. When they pulled into the winding drive, Carla clutched Sherry. "This is it! But it's all dark. We can't go up there!"

Joel took the curving road to the side of the mansion and hit the brakes. Three cars blocked the drive at a side door. He shoved into reverse, the car moved, and two men leaped from the doorway shouting, "Stop!"

A revolver gleamed and Joel slammed on the brakes.

One of the men flashed a badge. "Federal Narcotics. What is your business here at this hour?"

They all talked at once. Joel's explanation convinced the officers that he was responsible for alerting the police to Lynn's kidnapping. "This friend of ours, Kurt, who was in

140

the wreck gave me these addresses. I've never been here before."

The officers questioned each one. Then one of the agents instructed, "Pull your car back a few yards, as close to the bushes as you can. We might have to use the drive. By the way, do any of you know a girl from Philly — Jodi Lam — "

"Yes!" they responded in chorus.

"Did you know she was found dead of — "

Carla's cry brought the officer's face closer to view. "I'm sorry, but we need your help in convicting the one or ones responsible. Now, since you know this slick operator, Hal Chase, you can help us question him.

"You boys step outside with me. When Hal comes out, I want you to confront him with this statement: 'Jodi Lambert is dead, Hal Chase.' That's all I want you to do. We'll take it from there. And not a sound from this car, no matter what happens. Get me?"

"We'll do our best, sir," Joel assured him.

Gil brushed a kiss on Julie's cheek and left. His whisper, "Don't worry, girls," brought a sharp retort from Sherry.

"Don't worry, he says. Wow! What have we gotten ourselves into!"

"Quiet!" Julie tried to see through the darkness ahead. "Here comes someone."

They watched the officers halt and question one after another, as more police cruisers arrived to pick up the suspects.

"There's Hal now!" Sherry gasped. They watched, fascinated. He waved his arms back and forth. His voice was muffled by the swish of rain that the wind beat against the car.

Then Joel and Gil stepped forward. In the pale light Hal registered shock; his body went rigid; his head shot up; he froze like a statue.

Then Hal was ushered into a police car and the boys came running back.

Gil laughed, "That was faked, if you ask me."

"What?" the girls demanded.

"His surprise when we said Jodi was dead. Don't you think he knew it already, Joel?"

141

"I'd say so, Gil. His reaction was too dramatic. He's slick, all right. Smooth as oil."

An officer bent down to their window. "Thank you, boys. I'd advise you to go straight back to Philadelphia and leave the search to us. We'll do everything possible to locate this Lynn Hale. If she's in New York tonight, we'll find her."

Joel backed out and swung into a lighted boulevard. The car was strangely quiet.

When they reached the tunnel, Carla began to cry. "Jodi! What *happened* to you?"

Lynn opened her eyes. A doctor was listening to her heart. "Complete exhaustion," she heard him mutter.

"How did I get here?" She tried to sit up, but the doctor shook his head and the nurse pressed her back gently. "Where am I?"

"In Mercy Hospital, Miss. Your brother said you'd knocked yourself out sightseeing in the big city. He felt safer leaving you here for a day or two while he takes care of some business. He said you would understand, Miss — let me look at the chart again — Miss Mary Myers."

The nurse held out a pink pill and a glass of water. "Take this, Mary, and we'll see about some hot soup. How long has it been since you have eaten anything?"

Lynn tried to remember. It had been an eternity since breakfast. "What time is it now?" she asked weakly.

"Almost two o'clock in the morning. You kids go too fast these days. But we'll have you tuned up here in no time. A little food — and you must have had a hard fall. Your back is bruised. We'll take x-rays later on today. Your brother said to take good care of you, Mary."

"I should call home! Eemah will — "

"Let's take it easy now. I'm sure your brother will take care of that for you. What would you like to eat?"

The hot lunch gave Lynn new strength, but she was so drowsy. She tried to concentrate, but sleep closed in.

In the morning she awoke with a start. A different nurse stood by her bed with a thermometer. While Lynn held it in her mouth, a nurse's aide paused in the doorway and smiled at her. She held a sheaf of newspapers.

142

Lynn nodded and looked around for her purse. Oh, no! The plastic envelope. What had that stranger named Bobby given her? She removed the thermometer long enough to say, "My purse is — " and the aide tossed a paper on her table, saying, "Take it. I'll be back later and you can give me the dime then."

Lynn laid the paper beside her. Why had they called her *Mary?* Oh, yes. Bobby didn't know her name — had never met her before. How would she get out of that? They would no doubt ask her more questions today. Name and address? Parents?

The nurse took the thermometer. "You're doing fine, Mary. It's normal. Do you think you could sit up for breakfast? How about this easy chair over here, while I make your bed? Careful."

Lynn swung her feet down. She had never felt so stiff and sore and tired in her whole life.

The nurse placed a light blanket over her knees and picked up the paper. "Huh! Big headlines." She glanced at the front page. "Big picture on the front page. I'll have to look at it later. Here."

Lynn took the paper, laid it face up on her lap, and her heart raced. The picture was of her and Hal! She looked hysterical and Hal stood beside her, his mouth open and his eyes wild.

Lynn darted a quick look at the nurse and looked down at the paper again. *Narcotics Raid in Millionaire Playboy's Mansion. Bobby King* — Lynn stared at his photo. It was the handsome young man who had helped her escape! She read as fast as she could. Bobby owned that estate and was wanted for questioning in the death of his current fiancée, *Jodi Lambert*, who was found in her car on Park Avenue in upper Manhattan *dead of an overdose of drugs.*

Tears crept down Lynn's cheeks. She brushed them off quickly, and when the nurse gave her bed a final pat, Lynn answered with a smile. "I'd like to sit up for breakfast."

"Of course, Mary. That's a good sign you are making a fast recovery. We'll have you home in no time. Which reminds me — I have some paper work to get done. After you have eaten, I'll bring my chart and we can fill in the necessary details."

Lynn watched the white shoes padding across the room. Her heart raced. She must get out of this place at once! She crossed to the table and shakily opened the drawer. There was her plastic envelope. The roll was thick. A quick search showed the bills were all tens and twenties. Bobby had given this to her because he hated it. It had cost him his health and might cost him his *life!* No wonder he wanted to leave town. If Jodi had died because of his —

Lynn removed her street clothes from the closet, slipped from her hospital gown, and dressed. She found a paper sack, put the plastic envelope inside, and stepped to the door. No one was in the hall, and there was an exit sign to her left.

She glided to the door, sped down two flights, and walked slowly along the corridor. As she passed the cafeteria, her legs began to shake. She was weak and hungry.

She located an exit door and walked down a circular drive.

Relief shot through her body as she saw a taxi parked near the hospital entrance. The driver held the door for her.

28

"Where to, lady?" The driver was looking at Lynn.

"Oh! Why — the bus — no. You have a train stop here, don't you?"

"Yes, ma'am."

That settled it. She couldn't go home now anyway. She couldn't face Philadelphia tomorrow after they saw the Sunday papers. "Train station," she said.

She would have to take time to eat; she was getting too weak to stand. The coffee shop looked inviting. Lynn

144

ordered, then fled to the rest room to inspect her dress. The mirrors reflected her disheveled appearance.

She dashed cold water on her face. Would the hospital connect her picture in the paper with her disappearance? No, the picture did not look like her. But her friends back home would know! Someone had given her name. Under the second headline it said *Lynn Hale, high schooler from Philadelphia, under influence of LSD*. And she looked it! No one would ever believe her story.

She tried to smooth her hair. No comb. She looked horrible! How much money was there? No one was around. She thumbed through the bills. One hundred, twenty, forty, sixty, eighty — there must be at least five hundred. The way she looked this morning, someone would think she had stolen it. *I can't take a ten dollar bill from a sack and pay for my meal!*

She stumbled back to her table, sat down, and leaned her head on her hands.

The coffee brought a flicker of life, and her hands and feet grew less numb. The waitress was cheerful. "Here are your bacon and eggs. Choice of apple or raspberry jelly for your toast."

Lynn slid a bill across the table. "Please — I'm in a hurry to catch a train. Would you change this for me now — to save time?"

"Sure." The girl rang her sale and brought back the change. Lynn left a quarter on the table and put the rest in the sack. She began to feel better.

In the station she found packaged raincoats for sale. She bought a billfold, enclosed one of the bills, deposited her plastic envelope in the large raincoat pocket, and walked to the ticket window with confidence.

"Yes, Miss?"

She had no idea where to go. Glancing up at the table on the wall, she read Trenton — Philadelphia. Another column listed Lakewood — Atlantic City. She had visited Atlantic City one summer and had always wanted to go back. She said, "One way to Atlantic City, please. And could I stop this afternoon in Lakewood, over Sunday?"

145

"Certainly. I'll make out the ticket."

She decided to buy the necessary clothing, purse, and a small piece of luggage in Lakewood. Before she looked for work down in Atlantic City, she would have to rest until she was stronger.

The train clicked soothingly south through the State of New Jersey. Lynn closed her eyes and saw herself lying on a beach towel among scores of vacationers along the crowded seashore. *I'll blend with the scene and sleep for days.*

She was too tired to think. The shock of seeing the morning paper glazed her mind with horror. No one would ever believe her story of what had happened. Sherry and the others would never speak to her again.

From the station in Lakewood she took a taxi to a shopping center and purchased the things she would need. An hour later she was one of the well-dressed shoppers who thronged the mall.

At a beauty salon she made an appointment for late afternoon. Then she deposited her new suitcase and beach bag at a hotel, ate a bowl of chili in the coffee shop, bought a Philadelphia Sunday paper, and went to her room. The story was front-page news, although it did not make the top headlines.

The story continued on the second page, and she cried aloud. Someone had given the papers her senior picture. Underneath the photo she read: *This attractive teen-ager, Lynn Hale, of Howard High School, was found at the mansion with Hal Chase.*

At the beauty salon she asked about having her hair dyed. Would they have time to do it on a Saturday night?

The beautician suggested a color rinse. The girl who did her shampoo sighed, "Why do you want to change it? If I had gorgeous hair like yours, I'd be proud of it."

You wouldn't be proud if you were in my shoes. Lynn's bright red-gold hair dulled to a coppery brown, and her long, swinging hair style became bangs and a shorter blunt cut effect. She smiled at the transformation. Perfect! No one would recognize her from the photo now.

In her hotel room Lynn pushed a chair to the window facing the avenue and sat looking out. The room was dark, and street signs blinked on and off while her thoughts flashed with them.

An aching loneliness began to gnaw through the numbed areas of her soul. The ache constricted her throat; stifled sobs shook her body. With bitterness she recalled the recent days. How could life be so hard? Everything had gone against her. It was too much to bear.

She would decide now — tonight! Either she would go her own way and plan her own life from here — or she would trust God to work it out His own way. Tears rained down, blurring the street scene. She leaned her head against the window frame. It was hard to suffer because of others — first for Joel's unfaithfulness, then for Kurt's infatuation, and finally for Pauline!

Her eyes opened wide as she stared through the space of centuries, comprehending. *On a rugged hill stood a rugged cross* . . . Her Lord had hung on a hard wooden frame when He took the punishment for *her* — for *everyone! He bore our sins in His own body on the tree* . . .

"He suffered for *my sin*," she whispered.

Lynn sobbed, "Oh, God, You've known my every thought! I can't hide from You. I'm sorry for all my sinful thoughts."

Communion was restored as she surrendered her heartache to Him. *If we confess our sins, He is faithful and just to forgive us our sins, and to cleanse us from all unrighteousness.*

She wandered to the dresser, turned on a lamp, and picked up the large Gideon Bible. She turned the pages lovingly, glancing at a verse in Leviticus. *I . . . have severed you from other people, that ye should be mine. . . .* God's Word to the children of Israel, and to *her!*

Her legs began to shake. God had set her free! When her whole world was crashing, when all friends and family had forsaken her, God was still faithful. He was all she needed.

Lynn bowed her head; the comfort of His presence brought a deep peace. Her first impression was the conviction that she should get in touch with the Stones. Eemah would be so worried when she heard the bad news.

Lynn wrote a note on hotel stationery. If she mailed it in the morning, they would receive it Tuesday.

"Dearest Eemah, Please don't worry. The papers are all wrong about me, and I'll try to explain as soon as I get back, but I need a long vacation. I'm terribly tired. I may go south for awhile, but don't know just where I'll stay yet — depends on where I find work. Thank you more than I can say for all your kindness to me. I love you and — remember — God loves you. I'll phone as soon as I get settled somewhere. Love to you all, Lynn."

She must write Miss Lindy also; she was a true friend. Lynn arranged writing materials on the bed and leaned against the pillows in the dark. She would write after awhile.

The street lights flickered red and green across the ceiling; a faint aroma of popcorn was wafted through the open window. Lynn felt the load lifted; it was such deep relief to get everything settled. She slept soundly.

Atlantic City was a disappointment. Room rent was high and Lynn was too tired to look for work. Rain and cloudy skies confined her to the small, dreary tourist room for a week.

By Saturday she was restless and eager for a change. The church page of the newspaper listed pastors and subjects for Sunday morning's sermons. She chose one and walked to church Sunday morning.

In the foyer she picked up advertising folders from various Bible colleges and spent the afternoon reading them. One sounded inviting: "Come to Hudson Taylor Bible College near scenic Chattanooga, Tennessee." The color photos of the Great Smokies stirred a responsive chord. They were almost as beautiful as her Blue Ridge Mountains.

She decided to take a bus to Chattanooga, look for work, and inquire at the college.

The trip was pleasant and Lynn's spirits revived. A quietness and assurance of heart convinced her that God was leading. The following Friday she was enrolled in summer school at Taylor College, had office work to help with her support, and had a cheerful room overlooking a skyline of low, wooded mountains. The same evening she called the Stones.

Eemah answered. "Leen, darling! How could you be giving us such worriment? Your father has been all over looking for you already! Even the police couldn't trace you. Where have you been keeping yourself, darling? Look! Give me your telephone number and your address quick! I call your father for you and he calls you right back.

"What *happened?* Your girl friends keep asking me 'has she called — has she written another letter?' I am saying she doesn't let me know already.

"And Leen —" Eemah's voice broke. She was crying. "Mine Gil — he has moved away! He is believing this Jesus and Sammy told him he could not stay with us any longer. Oh, what did we ever do that this should happen to us? We are heartbroken, Leen. Oy, I should live so long to see this! It's that girl friend of yours — the Evans girl — and her brother that have changed his mind about us. I don't want that I should ever see them —"

"Eemah! Listen!" Lynn heard a sob and kept talking. "No one turned Gil against you, dearest Eemah. I've heard Gil say many times that you two mean everything to him. And he is too intelligent to let someone merely 'change his mind.' Are you listening? Good. I want to tell you something. God is real, and you can only know Him by knowing the One He sent to earth, Jesus, your Messiah. He saved me in a miraculous way from hoodlums that kidnapped me —"

Eemah cried, "We heard all about how they kidnapped you, darling. Sherry and Carla came over, and they told me to tell you already they were praying for you to write to them. They want that I should tell you how much they love you and miss you and *I miss you,* Leen. Why don't you come back here and go to college? We have *nobody!*" Her cry reached Lynn's heart.

"Call Gil and let him come home, Eemah. Let him explain *why* he believes in Jesus. Give him this chance. I'm certain that will make you feel better. Eemah —"

"Leen, we are Jewish. I was born a Jew and will die a

149

Jew. But enough of this foolishness. Your father is frantic and I must call him now. You are writing me every week, mine daughter! And I am telling the girls you are calling and that you are all right, darling."

Lynn bowed her head as she stood by the phone. The girls missed her! They still cared! Could it be true?

The phone rang again and her heart thumped. Her father!

Finally she answered. He said, "Lynn —" and his voice broke. "I must see you! I've got to *know* you are all right." The tenderness in his tone sent her back several years to the loving home life they had once shared.

She started to say, "I'm sorry about —" but he interrupted, "I understand. Please — don't worry about explaining. I want to come down on a little vacation trip to see you. I've been ready to leave ever since Mrs. Stone received your letter from Lakewood."

29

LYNN FLEW DOWN the hall to her room, singing.

The phone rang again, and a girl called, "For you, Lynn."

She ran back to the hall phone. The girl smiled from her door. "You're popular tonight."

Lynn lifted the receiver and thrilled at the sound of Sherry's excited soprano.

"Lynn, dear, *dear* Lynnie! Why did you disappear? Do you know the police couldn't even trace you? We're all dying to know what happened!

"So you're at Taylor? Oh, Lynn, do you think I'd be accepted for the fall term? I'm just terribly lonesome. Carla just started dating Ron and Julie's going up to Nyack. She and Gil are floating on cloud a hundred and nineteen and can't bother to look down on us ordinary mortals. Really? You think I could come down there?

"And, Lynn, I've got to tell you *everything!* I'll pay the folks for this call, even if it's ten bucks. Did you know Kurt was saved?"

Lynn held her breath as Sherry described their flying trip.

"And, Lynn, Joel, Julie, Gil, and I went upstate to the hospital where he was taken. I asked Kurt where he would have landed if he'd been killed in that wreck, and he said he knew it wouldn't be heaven. And he cried — *real tears!*

"Joel talked to him too, and all four of us were there when he asked God to save him. He said now he knew the difference between Satan's deadly gate to paradise which leads to hell, and the one-way gate, Christ the Lord, to God and His heavenly home.

"Now, Lynn, just listen to this. Julie sat in the back seat with me all the way up to the hospital and back, and she told me some things you'll be interested to hear — about Natalie. That conceited thing acted so pious in public — wouldn't let Joel even hold her hand when they were around church — never raised her voice above a throaty mumble, and everyone thought she was great! So *refined!*

"But the Evans's soon discovered what she was. She stayed in bed real late at their house and whined to Julie that she didn't feel like coming down to breakfast, and would she please tell her brother to bring her up a tray. Julie mentioned this to me — which shows what an impact it made on her.

"And Mrs. Evans began to see through that gal. Joel admits that he was infatuated, but Julie told me he said he never did love Natalie. She started acting as though they were engaged — said she thought people of *their* class were not expected to serve the Lord except with their money and church attendance. Julie says she talked constantly of her dad's wealth and prestige, and she told Joel she would never consider living in anything less than a modern home that they could 'use for entertaining' — and that was *her* ultimate in serving the Lord. Wow!

"Did I tell you about Joel's decision to go into the ministry? Well, his family caught on after awhile that Natalie would make a lousy minister's wife. And Julie hopes he will marry you, Lynn. What do you think of that!"

Lynn could hardly think of anything else the next day. She was thankful her father was visiting over the weekend when she could relax for a few hours from the strenuous summer school studies.

He surprised her Saturday afternoon as she sat studying in the shade of campus pines.

"Lynn!"

Her heart ached for him; he looked tired and ill. He clasped her close. How good it was to feel his scratchy coat against her cheek.

"Sit down on the bench, Dad."

He kept looking at her, love shining through the tears in his eyes. "Thank God you are safe and unharmed!" He looked down, hesitated, then continued, "I don't know how I could be so blind, Lynn. You are so gentle and sweet — exactly like your own mother.

"I trusted God to take care of you, honey, but I'll confess I was frantic. When the police were unable to follow any leads and you completely disappeared — that first weekend — I began to realize what you meant to me. I couldn't eat or sleep. That's when Bernice —"

She waited for him to go on. His voice sounded strained. "Ever since you left, Lynn, she had become increasingly high strung. Finally I knew something was radically wrong. Even Bette was afraid of her. I had to take her to several doctors before we found an answer.

"The night I paced the floor, worried about you, she went into actual fits. She threw things at me — and — well, to make it short, two doctors told me she is insanely jealous. She drove herself into a frenzy, and they recommended hospital treatment. It will take much psychiatric care to bring her out of this.

"Bette wanted me to take her to her grandparents. She will stay in Virginia with them until things get settled."

His voice broke. Lynn put her hand on his arm. He

152

stroked her hand and she saw the tears on his face. "Lynn, I hope you can forgive me. I was so blind."

"I understand, Dad. It's all in the past. Let's forget it and make a new start."

After her father returned to Philadelphia, Lynn received an air-mail letter from Kurt. As she read, a weight lifted from her; he had burdened her mind even in her dreams.

She read the words slowly, glad that no one was around to interrupt. "Lynn, if only I could have started our friendship with Christ in my heart! It would have been so different; you would not have suffered so much on my account.

"Lynn, I was the cause of Craig's death. If God wasn't willing to forgive me, I could never live in peace. But thank God I have peace through Jesus Christ our Lord — Jesus Christ, our bridge to heaven. Joel and Gil have talked by the hour to me. And Sherry scolded me, bless her. God sent her to visit me at the right time and I'll thank Him forever. You girls all proved to me there is a God in heaven. Sherry believes Joel led Craig to Christ. I hope so — with all my heart. God has taken away all the bitterness, Lynn. Now I know what Carla meant about changed attitudes.

"Does it sound strange to hear me talk like this? It was God's wonderful grace that saved me. He rescued me from the power of darkness.

"Hal and Bobby were bailed out, but they are two of the most miserable people you'll find. Bobby's millions haven't given him one ounce of peace in his heart or the joy of the Lord which I found when Jesus Christ tuned me in to God. Oh, Lynn! The Bible is a new Book since I have the Holy Spirit of God to open my eyes. Now I understand what you kept trying to tell me.

"And now, Lynn, precious friend, I trust God to put it in your heart to forgive me. If only I could undo all that was done! I'd like to try to tell you in a few words, if I can, what made me think the way I did.

"Basically, guys like Hal and I are searching for the answers. If we had been brought up in a church like Grace which has the answer to what life's all about, we might not

153

have wandered into this thing. But we weren't. Our church is like Gil's — a form of ceremony and ritual — absolutely no spiritual life to kindle a spark of interest toward God.

"You can see why fellows like Hal and I fell for the ballyhoo about our ancestors being a bunch of long-faced Puritans and hypocrites. They emphasize the *Paulines* in the church and neglect the joyful Christians. And until I experienced this joy of the new birth, I thought of Christianity the same way.

"Lynn, I have a burden for these hippies because I know what makes them think as they do. So many of these intellectuals declare they have gone through life looking for something meaningful and thought they would find it in the universities. But the ungodly professors uproot their basic belief in God, they set guys like Hal adrift from former faith and family ties, and leave them to roam the earth searching.

"Some of Joel's classmates have visited me and shown concern for these guys adrift. I expect to major in music this fall and join their singing group. We are plotting a counter-attack on Satan's stronghold. We're going to work and pray, and we're hoping to sing our way into the lives and hearts of college kids. I believe God can use us to reach some."

The weeks and months flew. Sherry came to Taylor and she and Lynn enjoyed a close friendship.

Then Christmas vacation arrived. Lynn's father sent her train fare to come home for the holiday vacation, and Sherry traveled with her.

This time the house at 36007 was alive with welcome. Her father introduced Mrs. Peterson, his housekeeper, an elderly widow whom Lynn remembered from their church. She had the kitchen bulging with Swedish cookies and cakes.

Mrs. Evans phoned the day after Lynn arrived. "We want you folks over for dinner. Gil's family said they could come too, Lynn. Isn't that an answer to prayer? They have changed their minds about his engagement to Julie and love her as they do you, dear. Lynn, is it all right with you if we make this a reunion of your Bible club friends? Good. And now someone over here wants to talk with you."

Lynn's heart raced until Julie's voice reached her. "Oh, Lynn! Lynn! How wonderful to hear your soft voice again. Honey, I can hardly wait to tell you all about Gil and me. You heard about it? Oh, that Sherry! She would! But she hasn't told you everything. I can hardly wait to see you; I want to tell you something. Well, I'll tell you right now — I'm on the upstairs phone and no one is around — Joel is over at Miss Lindy's.

"Lynn, I almost think he would run the opposite direction if he saw you — he feels so rotten about the way he let you down. But he has never forgotten you. Just listen to this. He confided that a long time ago Miss Lindy helped him see things in true perspective. He asked her — even when he was dating Natalie — how he could be sure you were the one God had chosen for him; his heart said you were the one he loved.

"But, Lynn, he is sure you would never look at him again! He said you two were actually engaged to be married! Lynn, I never *knew* that!"

"We had an understanding —" Lynn stopped. Someone was ringing the doorbell. "I'll call you back, Julie. Someone's at the door."

Miss Lindy handed Joel a plate of cookies. He chewed one absently, pacing across the room, and she said tartly, "What's the matter, young man? Aren't you enjoying your vacation?"

"Miss Lindy —"

"Yes?"

"When I came home in October you said that — that you knew Lynn was — Well, what I mean is, I asked you then if you had heard from her, and if you thought she was going with any boy at Taylor, and you thought she was interested in someone here because you knew she was writing someone in Philly. Can you tell me any more now. I suppose she has called you."

"Yes, Joel, I'm afraid you have had some competition. She's been writing faithfully every week!"

"Who?"

Miss Lindy replied confidently, "Why don't you ask *her*

about it? Or you might take a look at these, if you need a little light on the subject."

Joel thumbed through a stack of letters. *Miss Melinda Mapes,* in Lynn's handwriting! Miss Lindy's sparkling eyes were crinkling at the corners.

He laughed, relaxing in a glow of relief. "Do you think she'd —"

Miss Lindy pointed to the door. "I think — if I were you — I'd not waste any more time *thinking!*"

He bolted from the house and out to his car.